THE EMPTY BOOTH
AT
INDIAN MARKET

THE EMPTY BOOTH
AT
INDIAN MARKET

LINDA A. MORTON

ISBN: 979-8-218-61454-6

Interior design and formatting by:

E.M.
TIPPETTS
BOOK DESIGNS

www.emtippettsbookdesigns.com

CHAPTER 1

The artist drove to the Santa Fe Convention Center on this Friday morning of Indian Market weekend. He had just driven six hours from the reservation in Arizona for this yearly event. The artist followed the signs that read *Juried Exhibition Entries*. He parked his van in the lot and took the paper that had notified him of his acceptance to the juried show. After stretching his legs a bit, he got the dolly out of the van. He carefully unloaded the crate with his bronze sculpture titled *Desert Farmer*. This is the piece he had hoped would win a prize.

The artist took his sculpture into the Convention Center lobby and saw a sign at a table that read *Register Entries Here*. He presented his paperwork to the Committee person and was given a receipt telling him his booth number for the weekend. Booth number 35.

As he carefully pushed the dolly through the Convention Center, he observed other artists setting up their entries. Maybe he would see his Mentor, Evelyn, here today. She was coming from the same village in Arizona.

The artist followed the signs leading to the section named *Sculpture*. He showed his receipt to the person directing the artists. He was shown a table to set up his entry and was given a 8xll inch cardboard sign with his name, tribal affiliation, title of the entry and booth number. The artist unloaded the bronze from the crate and set it on the table. He placed the sign under the mahogany mount that held the bronze in place. The artist spoke to the piece like a proud parent. "You represent Bacavi Village and all the desert farmers of the Hopi Reservation. You will do us proud."

The artist looked around the Hall. There was one-half hour left before judging began and the room was bustling with activity. Today, there would be a luncheon of judges, then collectors who were invited to preview the show, and later in the evening there would be a gala event. His bronze would be viewed by many even before he set up his booth. Any interested collectors would remember his name and come to his booth to see more of his work.

He found his friend and Mentor, Evelyn, along with her daughter at a nearby table. He admired her bronze of a Hopi woman with painted jewelry. Painting bronze was a skill the artist hoped to learn someday.

"Let's meet for dinner tomorrow night after the Market." The artist suggested.

Evelyn agreed. "Let's meet at my hotel at 6:30 p.m. They have a great restaurant with Native cuisine. Many of the artists stay there."

As he was leaving the Exhibition Hall, the artist stopped to admire the other artwork displayed. He had read that over 200 tribal affiliations were represented here. It might be his only chance to see it, since he'd be at his booth most of the weekend.

He put the dolly back in the van and looked for a drive-through restaurant. He found a place selling burgers on Guadalupe Street and ordered a green chile cheeseburger and fries. He ate in his van and thought of where he would spend the night. He didn't have a hotel reservation and knew hotels would be booked this weekend, especially near downtown Santa Fe. He had a pillow and blanket, so decided to sleep in his van.

After eating, he drove back to the area by the Convention Center and saw Public Parking on Marcy Street, across from the Convention Center. He thought it would be convenient, since his booth was on Marcy Street. The hourly rate was high but it had overnight parking. He decided to go sight-seeing around the outskirts of Santa Fe and return later in the evening.

The artist drove up the famous Canyon Road and parked. He decided to look for galleries that might want to represent his work. After a two-hour search, he returned to his van with names and contact information. He proceeded up Camino del Monte Sol and drove past the historic estates of long-gone early Santa Fe artists. He proceeded to St. John's College Campus and Atalaya Hill. He parked the van and walked to the Student Center. He sat in the air-conditioned Center and observed the comings and goings of student activity while sipping on a cold soda. He hadn't gone to college and wondered what it would be like.

The artist drove to Sun Mountain and over to Old Santa Fe Trail. From there, he merged onto Old Pecos Trail and proceeded to the Interstate. He would drive to Galisteo and have dinner at an old Hacienda he read about. This area had resident artists whose work was displayed there.

By seven p.m., the artist had viewed local artwork and enjoyed a meal of chicken enchiladas with the famous Hatch green chile. The artist returned to Santa Fe and observed the sky as it began to change colors, from blue to pink and orange. During the hour's drive back to the downtown area, the sun had made its descent.

Downtown Santa Fe on this Friday evening was filled with visitors and locals going to restaurants and the Convention Center's Gala Event. The artist rolled down his window and inhaled the cool mountain air. It was refreshing after a hot day in August at this high desert elevation.

He entered the City Parking Lot and found a space near Marcy Street. After parking the van, the artist called his sister in Bacavi. She had encouraged him to enter this juried show at the largest gathering of American Indian Art in the world.

"The drive was fine and I entered *Desert Farmer* in the show. There's a lot of great work here. I'm staying in my van tonight, since it's close to the booth and near the Convention Center." The artist noticed someone standing outside the van's passenger window. The man looked aggressive with his furrowed brow and eyes glaring at the artist. "Wait a minute." The artist told his sister.

Suddenly, the stranger started pounding on the passenger window. "Money! Give me money!"

"No! Go away! Go away!" Yelled the artist. "No money!" The man left and the artist resumed his phone call.

"Sorry, but someone was begging for money. He's gone now. "He heard the concern in his sister's voice and tried to reassure her. "I'm in a public lot across from the Convention Center. I should be safe here. I'll call you tomorrow after the Market." The artist hung up. He made sure his doors were locked and rolled out his bedding. It was a long day and he had two days to sell his artwork at the Market. He needed some rest.

The next morning, the artist awoke early. He felt stiff after sleeping on the van's hard floor the night before. He stepped out of the van on this quiet Saturday morning. In a couple of hours, the area would be packed with visitors. He splashed some water on his face and toweled off. He unloaded his table and a chair and went in search of his booth.

He found his booth #35 and set up his chair and table. He was one of the only artists out at seven a.m. He went back to the van and got another folding chair and his binder with his resume and photos of other works to show potential collectors. He locked the van, dropped off the chair and binder at the booth and went to look for a Food Truck or restaurant. He needed strong coffee to start the long day ahead.

He turned onto Lincoln Avenue and proceeded to Palace Ave. He spotted a Food Truck. They were just getting set up, but coffee was ready. He ordered a burrito and fry bread, then took his coffee to sip as he looked around the Plaza. He saw a Navajo man setting up Sandpaintings for an elder. There were Zuni Pueblo Indians setting up a booth on Palace Avenue. The artist knew the Zunis were famous for their Squash Blossom jewelry designs in turquoise. Soon, American Indian artists from all over the country would fill this downtown center.

His breakfast was ready to pick up and he looked for a place to sit. He found a fire hydrant on the corner. Good enough. The artist savored the burrito with green chile and decided to save the fry bread for later. As he was finishing his last bite, he noticed someone walk past. The man looked familiar, but didn't look like an exhibitor. He looked mad and wild as he flapped his arms up and down while turning in circles. The artist stood up and looked around for a Security Guard or police. He went to the Plaza, but didn't see an officer. When he returned, the unruly man was gone.

The artist decided to return back to Marcy Street and saw two Navajo men in a booth across from his. He introduced himself and said "Man, I just saw a strange guy who looked like he might be on drugs. He has long brown hair, an Anglo. He's messed up, so be careful if you see him. I'm looking for an officer to report it. If you see Security, tell them what I said, OK?"

The Navajo men nodded in affirmation and continued setting up their booth. The artist walked to the Convention Center to use the facilities. It was eight a.m. and it would be hours before he had a break. He saw a woman at the Information Counter inside and asked if there was a Security Guard nearby. "No, not yet. They should be here soon."

"When you see a guard, tell him there's a man, an Anglo man about six feet tall, long brown hair, messy. He's wearing black pants and a white tee shirt. He's acting like he's on drugs or something. It's bad for the Market and not safe. They need to get him out of here. Be sure to tell someone, OK?" The artist insisted.

"OK, I will. The Police Station is two blocks away on Lincoln if you want to go file a complaint." The woman said.

The artist decided he would set up his booth and try not to worry about the strange man. As his moccasins hit the concrete pavement, he already missed the soft clay and sand of the reservation. As the artist proceeded to the parking lot, he suddenly remembered where he had seen the stranger. The man came to his van last night begging for money. He pounded on the window while the artist was talking to his sister.

He saw his white van and got his keys out. He unlocked the passenger door, then opened the side panel. He lifted the dolly and set it on the ground. He needed it to transport his heavy bronzes in their crates. The artist then stepped into the van and picked up the first crate. He spoke to it proudly. "OK, dear, it's your time to shine."

He turned to exit the van and saw a man holding the metal dolly up in the air. "No! No! Help!" yelled the artist. Before he could duck, the dolly hit him in the face. The artist dropped the crate on the ground and fell back inside the van. He looked up and saw the face of the attacker. It was the same man he saw last night and in the street this morning.

The attacker said something inaudible, then picked up the bronze that fell out of its crate and hit the artist on the head. The pain was sharp. He felt blood oozing onto the van's carpet. He saw a large shape hover over him reaching into his pockets. The artist didn't have the strength to push back. The light dimmed to darkness as the Hopi Indian prayed to his guardian spirit before losing consciousness.

The attacker took the man's wallet and found one hundred dollars and a gas card. He grabbed something from the dashboard. On the passenger seat, he saw fry bread on a napkin and grabbed that, too. He stumbled out of the van and closed the side panel door behind him.

The attacker put the small object in his pants pocket, along with the wallet. He wiped his bloody hands on his black pants. The fry bread would be his meal for today. He chewed it voraciously as he walked to Otero Street, then back up the hill.

CHAPTER 2

The new school year had just started for teacher, Laura Barnes, and she still wasn't quite ready to get back to work. Upon arriving home from walking her dogs along the Acequia, she thought about what she would do this lovely Saturday in August. She had seven hours before her fiance would arrive from Albuquerque. They had a dinner reservation at the Piano Bar on Water Street.

It had been over a year since they had met during the investigation of the gallery she worked at. Laura liked the man from the start and the feeling was mutual. When Laura's mother visited last summer, she met Marc and gave her parental approval. The couple began seeing each other whenever Marc could get a break from work. Being an FBI agent meant having an unpredictable schedule. Sometimes Laura would drive to Albuquerque for the day. This time, Marc was coming to Santa Fe.

Laura decided she would go downtown. This was Indian Market weekend, always a festive time of year in Santa Fe. She knew, of course, downtown would be crowded with collectors and tourists. Laura decided to walk, since parking would be nearly impossible. After feeding her pets, she grabbed her straw hat, sunglasses, purse and pepper spray.

She locked up the casita and walked over to Acequia Madre and its narrow sidewalks. Laura passed the adobe walls and flowered courtyards of the historic homes this quaint eastside neighborhood was known for.

As she approached the area called Gallery Row, she saw the gallery where she once worked. There was a sign on the door that read *Closed* in red letters. The building looked like an empty shell. It had been closed over a year now. Laura recalled the drumming and sound of singers in protest to the gallery owner's suspected theft of tribal burial items. Laura held onto her star pendant in memory of the young staffer that was killed. The Cherokee woman knew burial items were in the owner's collection. Hoping justice had been served, the teacher was glad she did what she could to help the investigation.

Laura took Alameda to Old Santa Fe Trail and observed people descending from all directions. She passed the La

Fonda Hotel, which had one of her favorite restaurants. She recalled the morning she and her mother met Marc for breakfast last summer. He wanted to meet her during her visit to Santa Fe. This place had a sentimental value for Laura.

As she walked through the crowds, Laura tried to get near the artists' booths. Though she didn't intend to buy anything, she enjoyed viewing the artistic creations. As a former Art Major in college, she appreciated art in many forms. This was the biggest American Indian Art Exhibit in the world and she wasn't going to miss it. She had read that to win a prize in this show could change the trajectory of an artist's career.

Laura saw a booth filled with Sandpaintings and an elder Navajo woman, Rosie, was explaining the healing property of one specific painting to a buyer. "The Medicine Man uses Sandpaintings to restore harmony and balance to a patient. The Medicine Man touches the painting then touches the patient to transfer medicine and power. As this is done, sickness falls from the patient. Before the sun sets, the Sandpainting is destroyed and the patient walks in harmony again." The elder pointed to different shapes and colors of the sand in the painting and their meaning. The buyer clearly appreciated the explanation and paid for the painting. Laura was impressed that this ancient tradition of healing was still being appreciated.

At another booth, Laura saw a man from Cochiti Pueblo sitting behind a table of fetishes, animal figures carved in stone. Some were big and some were small. Each animal had its' own traits. Laura admired the small owl. "How much for this one?" she asked.

"The wise one is $40.00. It is small so it can fit in your pocket or medicine bag." The man answered.

"Thank you. I will consider it." Laura replied.

Laura proceeded to another booth where she saw a petite woman with a lovely smile. Laura read the sign that said *Hopi artist, Evelyn S. from Arizona*. The two women exchanged greetings. Laura gazed at a bronze of a seated woman holding an empty bowl. The woman's eyes were closed and she had a serene smile, as if in meditation. "This is lovely." Laura told the artist.

"This is called *The Harmonious One*. She is in harmony with her world and her situation." Evelyn responded.

Laura thought of the stress of being a teacher and the elusive feeling of being in harmony. Laura looked at the price tag. $5000.00. "I love your work and wish I could take this home with me. I'm a teacher. I'm sorry I can't afford this."

"Here is my card. If you change your mind before Market ends, call me. I'll be in town until Monday noon. I'm Evelyn."

"You are very talented, Evelyn." Laura said while staring at the bronze. It was hard to divert her eyes. As she left the booth, she was amazed that a work of art had such a profound effect on her.

Laura proceeded over to the Palace of the Governors. It

was packed with layers of visitors pouring onto the street. People stretched their necks to get a look at the artwork under the portal.

Laura decided to get a soda and sit on a bench in the Plaza. She observed people in various attire. She saw rhinestone and denim jackets, fringed suede vests, cowboy hats and boots and lots of turquoise jewelry. A nearby booth had American Indian modern-day fashions. It was interesting to see young men and women wearing modern designs from an ancient heritage. One young woman had colored beads strung around her eyes.

Laura sat on the bench observing the diversity of the scene before her. There were the young and the old, the modern and traditional, the locals and the tourists. She enjoyed hearing the American Indian artists explain the spirit behind their work. Laura was so glad to be living in this cultural city. Though her hometown of Chicago was a great city, Laura felt comfortable in this small artistic community.

When she finished her drink, Laura walked toward Marcy Street. She saw a booth of wooden sculptures depicting graceful birds. She stopped to admire the heron. The artist was from the eastern band of Cherokee Indians. "I love your work. You really make the wood come alive." Laura said.

The artist smiled and said "Thank you. Take a flier with my resume and contact information." Laura took the flier and put it in her purse.

Next, she saw a booth of portraits of famous Indian leaders. Geronimo looked fierce, painted in purple and lime green. Sitting Bull sat stoic in reds and shades of orange. Laura nodded to the artist as she passed.

She passed an empty booth on Marcy Street, booth #35. The booth had a table, chairs and a binder on the table. She wondered why someone would leave the booth empty, since the Market was packed with visitors.

As she neared the Convention Center, Laura saw two police cars in the parking lot with their lights flashing. This public lot was filled with vehicles in town for the Market. She was curious and approached the scene. Laura recognized Santa Fe Police Chief Romero from the gallery investigation. He noticed her and waved her over. Laura saw yellow crime scene tape around a white van as she approached.

"Nice to see you, sir. It's been a while. Can you tell me what happened?" Laura asked.

"Laura, someone has been killed, beaten to death. That's all I can say now." The Chief replied.

"Was it someone here for the Market?" She asked.

"It looks like it. We have an insurance card, but no wallet or other ID. He had bronzes in his van. He was beaten with one of them. No suspects and Laura, we don't want to alarm the public." The Chief explained.

"Sir, I'm not sure if it's related, but there's an empty booth down Marcy Street. It's set up with table, chairs and a binder.

Maybe it was your victim's?" Laura suggested.

"It could be." The Chief called an officer over. "Officer, get your finger print kit and evidence bags and go with Ms. Barnes to the empty booth. Secure the binder. It might be the victim's."

"Yes, sir." The officer replied. He collected the supplies and followed Laura to the booth. As they walked, they heard whispers. *"What's going on? Do you know what happened?"*

Laura stepped aside as the officer put on gloves and opened the binder. He saw a resume with a photo of a man. It resembled the face of the badly beaten man in the van. He put the binder in the evidence bag. Laura stood by the evidence bag as the officer dusted the table and chairs for prints. He, then, secured the area with yellow crime scene tape.

Laura walked back to the parking lot with the officer. Some of the visitors stared but kept going. The officer addressed the Chief. "Sir, it looks like the victim had a booth here. He was setting it up, but never returned." The officer, still wearing gloves, took the binder out of the bag and opened it to the first page. "This is our victim, Raymond Sakitewa, from the Hopi Reservation in Arizona."

"Yes, it looks like it. The name matches the name on the Insurance card. There's a missing wallet, but the resume and the card can confirm his identity. Get the prints to the Lab." The Chief said.

"Thanks, Laura. That was helpful. We have an interstate

crime here. We're going to need your friend's help on this, you know." The Chief explained.

"He's planning on coming up for dinner tonight." Laura said, then wished she hadn't.

"I'll give him a call. He needs to contact the Hopi Reservation before he gets here. If I were you, I'd be flexible with those dinner plans." The Chief sounded slightly apologetic.

Laura already knew. "Yes, Chief. I understand."

CHAPTER 3

It was eleven thirty a.m. and Agent Bennett had just finished his work-out. He had the weekend free and was looking forward to seeing his fiancee in Santa Fe today. He had done laundry and went grocery shopping. He wanted frozen food on-hand so as not to waste perishables. In his line of work, he could be gone for days at a time.

He took a hot shower and got dressed. He was packing an overnight bag when his pager sounded. It was work. He called the office. "Marc Bennett here. I got your page."

"Marc, it's Agent Garland. I just got a call from Chief Romero in Santa Fe. He has a case he wants you to assist with."

"It's my weekend off, sir. Can it wait until Monday?" Marc

already knew the answer.

"The Chief wants you involved. You'll need to notify the Hopi Reservation. The victim is an artist who came to display at the Indian Market. Stop at the office on your way out and I'll give you more details." Instructed Agent-in-charge Garland.

"Yes, sir. I should be there within the hour." Marc said. "Thanks, Marc." Agent Garland hung up.

As he drove to the FBI office on Albuquerque's north side, Marc tried to recall if he knew any agents who were Hopi Indian. He had met officers in training seminars, but couldn't recall what their tribal affiliations were. He got to the office parking lot and called Laura.

"Laura, I'm still coming, but I've been called on a case up there. Hopefully, we can still have dinner at the Piano Bar later."

"It's all right, Marc. I saw Chief Romero and he told me he needed your help. I'll see you later." Laura said as she tried to hide the disappointment from her voice.

Marc entered the office building and found agent Garland in his office. "What do you have for me, Sir?"

"Hello agent. This morning, Santa Fe police found the body of Raymond Sakitewa, age 25. He was an artist preparing to show his work at Indian Market's. His booth was partially set up. The victim was found beaten to death in his van, which he might have slept in last night. It's located in the lot across from the Convention Center. Passers-by saw blood on the van's side panel door and a dolly on the ground next to it. It had blood on it, too. They called 911." Agent Garland explained. "The victim's face was badly beaten using a bronze sculpture. There was no wallet at the scene. The victim was identified by an insurance card in the van and a resume with his photo. The resume showed an address and phone number. Chief Romero sent me the contact information and asked that you contact the Hopi Reservation. The victim is from the Bacavi Village on the Third Mesa, Arizona. I'm forwarding this information to your e mail."

"OK, sir. I'll make the call. Do you know any agents out there?" asked Marc.

"No, I don't, but I'll ask around the office." Replied agent Garland.

Marc went to his office, pulled up the information on his e mail and printed it on paper. He, then, searched for the number of the Hopi Tribal Police. "This is Agent Marc Bennett with the FBI in Albuquerque. I need to talk to your Police Chief about a matter here, in New Mexico."

He was put on hold and a few minutes went by. "This is Chief George Shunpavy. How can I help you, agent?"

"Sir, I'm sorry to inform you that one of your Hopi residents has been killed in Santa Fe. I need you to help me contact his next of kin." Said the agent.

There was a long pause. "What is the victim's name and where was he found?" asked the Tribal Chief.

"The man's name is Raymond Sakitewa. He was found beaten to death in his van. He was there for the Indian Market. The Santa Fe police found a binder with his resume and photo in the booth he was setting up. They matched the photo to the victim. The van's insurance card had the same name. "Marc explained.

"This is very sad news, agent. Raymond is from generations of the Sakitewa clan in Bacavi. They are master dry farmers and have helped feed many of our people over the years. Raymond lived with his mother and his sister. He was considered one of the Hopi Tribe's top sculptors. I will notify the family. "Chief Shunpavy said.

"Sir, I'd like to contact whoever spoke to Raymond last. Maybe he said something that will help with the investigation. Will you give the family my number to call? I'm working with the Santa Fe police to find Raymond's killer." The agent asked.

"Agent Bennett, the Hopi are generally a peaceful people. We have a sacred covenant to live as peaceful and humble farmers, respectful of the land. For this reason, I don't think the killer is Hopi. I will give Raymond's sister your contact information."

"Thank you, and Chief, I'm sorry for your loss." The agent expressed his condolences.

Before leaving his office, Agent Bennett checked his gear: FBI vest, radio and batteries, handcuffs, ties, firearm, cell phone and charger. He picked up a handful of cards to hand out to witnesses.

On his way out, Bennett reported to the agent in charge. "Sir, I made contact with Hopi Tribal Police Chief George Shunpavy. He knows the victim's family. The victim was from a well respected and talented clan. The Chief does not think a Hopi would commit this crime. I'm leaving for Santa Fe now, sir."

"Agent, Chief Romero wants you to meet him at the Lincoln Avenue Police Station. From there, he will take you to the crime scene. He said it's a short walk."

"That's very brazen of the suspect to commit murder so close to a police station."

"Yes, it is. The suspect must have been out of his mind." Replied Agent Garland.

CHAPTER 4

It was early afternoon when Agent Bennett reached Interstate 25 heading north. Traffic was light. He looked out at the fields of Chamisa against the backdrop of the Sandia Mountains. The scent of Sage was in the air after a morning rain.

He passed Pueblo land before ascending La Bajada Hill. As his six-cylinder engine tugged a bit, he imagined the horses and buggies of old trying to get up this hill. The Model-T Fords would chug along slowly in the struggle to reach the top. Marc had read that the ascent was about a thousand feet.

Soon, the top of the hill and the edge of Santa Fe came into view. Elevation here was near seven thousand feet and the air was clearer than in Albuquerque. The trade-off was that the air was thinner, so Marc got a little more winded when exerting himself at the higher elevation.

In these wide-open spaces, Marc's imagination roamed. He imagined dinosaurs that once roamed the lush landscape when it was filled with lakes and rivers. Marc wanted to visit the Abiquiu Museum with Laura soon. He read that various smaller dinosaur bones have been found in that area and are on display at the museum. They could spend a weekend at the Ghost Ranch Retreat Center, where western movies have been filmed. He would mention it to Laura this weekend.

Marc approached the exit to Old Pecos Trail, the main artery to downtown Santa Fe. He exited the Interstate and noticed a new condo development on the right. The famous Pueblo Revival style of architecture had a backdrop of the Sangre de Christo Mountains. Marc enjoyed the open vistas of Santa Fe, since it had a restricted height limit on buildings. The mountains are the focal point here.

Upon merging with Old Santa Fe Trail, the traffic came to a crawl. Indian Market always brought a lot of visitors, so Marc knew Santa Fe would be busy. To avoid congestion, he took Paseo de Peralta over to Guadalupe Street, then around to Lincoln Avenue. He saw the parking lot of the Police Station and turned in. It was nearly 3 p.m.

Marc showed his badge to the officer at the front counter. "Marc Bennett here to see Chief Romero."

"He's expecting you. Right this way, agent." Replied the

officer.

"Thanks for coming, Marc. You know things get complicated when we have a crime involving someone from a sovereign nation. In this case, the Hopi Reservation. I appreciate the help from the FBI. Did you contact the Tribal Police?" Asked Chief Romero.

"Yes, sir. Chief George Shunpavy knew the victim and will notify the family. I asked for a relative to call me with more background information. Chief George doesn't believe a Hopi would commit such a violent crime." Marc explained.

"The crime scene is a short walk from here. Help yourself to water or coffee. We'll meet at the front desk and head over."

"Yes, sir." Marc went to freshen up, then got some coffee. Under his khaki vest, he wore his badge and firearm. Zip ties were in one pocket and phone in the other. He wore his running shoes, since he'd be doing a lot of walking this weekend.

The two men walked down Lincoln and turned on Marcy Street. There were booths set up along both sides of the street. Agent Bennett observed the crowd. Visitors were strolling and some were talking to the artists. Marc noticed the yellow tape around an empty booth. People seemed oblivious to the crime scene nearby.

The Chief spoke. "We're trying not to alarm the crowd due to the importance of Indian Market on state tourism. We did inform the Market Committee of what took place and they hired extra Security Guards who are stationed around downtown." The two men crossed the street near the Convention Center. They entered the parking lot.

Marc saw the white van surrounded by yellow crime scene tape. An officer stood nearby while a lab technician swabbed blood off the van's side panel and the dolly. Another technician dusted for prints and took photos. The bronze used in the murder had been dusted and bagged. A tow truck was parked nearby, waiting to haul the van to the crime lab.

"The Medical Examiner has the victim's body and is writing his report." The Chief explained.

Agent Bennett took out his phone and took photos of the van, the license plates and the front seat interior. He carefully walked near the side panel door, avoiding the lab technicians. He took a photo of the interior. He noticed an empty space on the dashboard where something once sat. The technicians were packing up their gear so the agent got a better view of the inside.

There was a large red patch on the beige carpet where the victim was found. He saw a pillow and blanket next to a crate. He took a photo.

Bennett asked "What do you think so far, Chief?"

"He had his booth partially set up. He was seen early when he got something to eat at the Food Truck. He told a Navajo elder in a booth across from his, to look out for a guy who looked like he was on drugs. If the Navajo saw a Security

Guard, he was to tell him to find this guy acting strangely. The artist never came back to his booth. It's booth #35. Looks like the victim slept in his van last night. That's about it. It would help if we got a match on prints from the lab." The Chief explained.

"Chief, I'd like to go interview the people who saw our victim this morning and interview others who may have seen something. I'll let you know if I learn anything new."

"Fine. I'll wrap up this crime scene and get the van towed to the lab." Said the Chief.

"I'll keep you informed." Marc said before walking into the crowd.

CHAPTER 5

Marc scanned the faces of the people he passed, looking for anything unusual. He saw the yellow tape around the booth on the right. Across from it, he saw two Navajo artists in a booth of Sandpaintings. He approached the elder. "Mr. Begay?"

"Yes, that's me." Replied the artist.

Marc showed his badge. "I'd like to ask you about the Hopi artist from booth 35." He, then, took out a pen and note pad.

"Like I told the officer, the Hopi artist was setting up early. He was here before we were." The elder motioned to the younger man next to him.

"What did he say to you?" The agent asked.

"He was on Lincoln Avenue, coming back from eating breakfast. He looked worried and came over to my booth. He said he was from that booth." The elder pointed to the taped area. "He said he saw a man acting like he was on drugs. He said the guy was Anglo, maybe six feet tall, messy long brown hair, black pants, white tee shirt. He told us to tell Security. Then, he walked down the street and never came back to his booth." The elder said.

"Do you know what time you saw him?" Marc asked.

"It was about eight o'clock. We just got here and were setting up. I'm glad I have my grandson here with me. We will be careful."

Marc gave the elder his card. "Can I get your phone number in case I have more questions?"

The Navajo elder pointed to his grandson. "This is Jerry Begay. You can have his number. I don't have a phone."

Marc wrote down the number and thanked the men.

As Marc walked, he looked for vendors who didn't have customers and approached. He showed his badge and asked if they saw anything unusual earlier in the morning. One vendor commented. "I heard someone yell *No! No!* but I couldn't tell where the voice came. There was a lot of commotion with people setting up booths, you know." The agent wrote down the artist's name and number.

"What direction did the voice come from?" Marc asked.

"It sounded like it came from near the Convention

Center." Marc thanked the artist.

Marc noticed a booth with a sign reading *Hopi artist, Evelyn S.* He waited until a customer left, then went to talk to the artist. "Excuse me, Evelyn." He showed his badge. "I'd like to ask you a few questions."

The woman looked surprised and cautious. "What's wrong, officer?"

"I see you are Hopi. Do you live in Arizona?" Marc asked.

"Yes, I do. I live in a village on Third Mesa. Why do you ask?" Evelyn replied.

"Do you happen to know an artist by the name of Raymond Sakitewa?" The agent asked.

The artist looked concerned. "Yes, I know Raymond. He's from my village, Bacavi. He is a student of mine. He's very talented. We thought he would win an award this year. You can see his work in booth #35."

"Did you drive here with Raymond or did he come in another vehicle?" Marc asked.

"Raymond drove by himself. The bronzes take up a lot of room. I drove with my daughter. She's here somewhere visiting friends. She relieves me every two hours so I can take a break. We're all going to meet for dinner later." Evelyn's brow furrowed. "Why are you asking me these questions? Is Raymond in trouble? Is he all right?"

The agent exhaled and delivered the bad news. "I'm sorry, Evelyn, but Raymond was killed this morning in his van. We don't have a suspect. I notified the Hopi Tribal Police and they will notify his family."

Evelyn's body weakened and she nearly fell back into the chair. She put her head in her hands and moaned. "Oh, Raymond. No, no, not Raymond." The artist was clearly distraught at the news.

"Evelyn, I'm leaving my card." He set it down on the table. "I would like to hear more about Raymond when you are ready to talk. I'm working with the police to catch his killer." Marc left the woman alone to grieve her loss.

CHAPTER 6

It was near 5 p.m. when Marc called Laura. "Laura, I'm running late. Can you make our dinner reservations for 7 p.m.? I hope to get to your place around 6:30."

"I'm glad you're nearby, Marc. I'll see you soon." Laura hung up.

The agent proceeded to walk the streets of downtown, being aware of anyone looking unusual. He noticed two police officers in the Plaza and stopped to talk. He showed his badge. "Hello, officers. Chief Romero called me in to assist in the murder investigation of the Hopi artist. The Food Truck vendor told police that the victim said he saw a disheveled man talking to himself this morning and wanted to alert Security. The victim told some artists near his booth the same thing."

"To be honest, agent, there are often transients and pan handlers around downtown. When we see them around the Plaza, we tell them to move on. They may return when the vendors are gone." Said Officer Randall.

"The victim described the man as six feet, light brown shoulder length hair and messy. Black pants, white shirt. He thought the guy might be on drugs." Marc described.

"Well, agent, that could be a few people around here. Some of these people camp in the hills, do drugs, then wander into town. If they're hallucinating, they could become violent." Replied Officer Manuel.

"Officers, I suggest you keep a wagon nearby and haul away anyone acting suspicious. Chief Romero and I will question them. Also, if you can talk to any of these kids or transients, ask if they know someone who had a bad drug experience this morning. Tell the other officers to do the same. Maybe we can get a lead." Marc shook hands with the officers before he left.

Marc needed a photo of Raymond, the victim. "Chief, can you send me a photo of Raymond Sakitewa to my phone? I need to show witnesses who may have seen him."

"The only good photo is the one on his resume." The Chief replied. "I'll blow it up and send it to you."

"Thanks, Chief." Marc hung up and continued walking. The Market was ending for the day and artists were packing up. Marc saw a Food Truck on Palace Avenue and waited until the customer left. His phone pinged and he saw a text with a photo. It was a photo of the victim.

"What can I get you?" asked the vendor.

"I'll take a root beer." Marc paid then showed his badge. "Sir, were you here early this morning around seven or eight?"

"Yes, I was here at seven. People are hungry and want breakfast before setting up their booths."

"Did you see this man this morning?" Marc showed the man the photo.

The vendor squinted at the photo. "Yes, I believe he was one of my first customers. He wanted coffee and had to wait ten minutes before I had burritos ready."

"About what time was that?" asked the agent.

"It was about 7:30 when I got his burrito ready. He wanted fry bread, too."

"Did you see him after that?"

"Well, there weren't many people here yet, so I did see him sitting over there on a fire hydrant." The man pointed. "He ate his food there. A little later, he got up and was looking around for someone. He seemed concerned about something he saw. Then, he came over and told me he wanted to find a Security Guard."

"Did he say why?" asked the agent.

"He said there was a guy who was yelling and acting strange. The artist was worried about what the guy might do.

He went looking for Security and I didn't see him again." The vendor replied.

"Ok, sir, can I get a phone number in case I need to follow up?"

"Sure, agent." They exchanged information.

Marc walked down Palace Avenue and asked other artists if they had seen the man in the photo. No one saw him.

The agent went to the Convention Center and approached the Information Desk. He showed his badge and asked "Were you here early this morning?"

The young woman responded. "Yes, I was here."

Marc took out his phone and displayed the photo. "Did you see this man here earlier?"

"He looks like the guy who came here earlier, like eight or eight thirty. One of the first visitors." She replied.

"How did he act, do you remember?" asked Marc.

"Well, he went to use the restroom. On his way out, he came to the desk. He seemed worried. He asked if there was a Security Guard he could talk to. I told him they were coming at nine. He said to have a guard come to his booth #35 right away."

Marc gave the woman his card and he wrote down her name and phone number. "Call me if you think of anything else."

Marc returned to the Police Station. It was nearly 5:30 p.m. and the Chief was still in his office.

"Sir, it helped having the victim's photo to show witnesses. Three witnesses said the victim was worried about someone or something he saw. He wanted to talk to a Security Guard. The last person he saw at the Convention Center said the victim wanted her to send Security to his booth 35 when they arrived. From the Convention Center, he went to his van to set up his artwork." Marc recapped his information.

"Also, Sir, I spoke to Officers Manuel and Randall in the Plaza. They said there's a problem with panhandlers around downtown. They told me people camp in the nearby hills, some do drugs, then wander into town. I was not aware of that." Marc said.

The Chief exhaled then explained. "Agent, we do have a problem with homelessness. It's worse in the warmer weather. People camp in the nearby hills and along the river in town. Some do drugs. We've had complaints. If we can, we pick them up and take them to a Shelter."

"Sir, we may have to look at this angle. Is there someone who can infiltrate the homeless population? Sometimes people talk about things they've done or seen." Marc suggested.

"Yes, I know what you mean. I can call the Shelter and ask the Director if there's anyone there who's willing to do us a favor. Good idea, agent." The Chief looked up a phone number.

"Sir, I'm staying in town until we catch this killer or

until Agent Garland calls me back. I'll be at the Market early Sunday to look around." Marc left the Police Station and got into his car.

Marc got into his Jeep and slowly drove through the downtown streets, then up the hill by Marcy Compound. Behind the Compound of condominiums, he saw a hillside adjacent to a wooded area. He drove around the Compound to a parking lot for visitors to the walking trails. He got out of his vehicle and walked up the hill where he saw a group of young people gathered behind the large white steel Cross. The agent saw colored tents set up in the woods. This would be easy access to downtown Santa Fe.

Marc went back to his vehicle and called Chief Romero. "Chief, I'm here behind the Cross of the Martyrs. There's a group of people laying in the grass and tents are set up in the woods nearby. When you find your informant, this is a good place to start."

"OK, agent. I'll have an officer parked at the bottom of the hill near the Paseo tonight and through the morning in case someone wanders off."

CHAPTER 7

Marc parked on Pena Court and retrieved his duffel bag. He rang the bell. "Well, hello, agent. Come on in." Laura answered.

"You look lovely, my dear." He gave her a big hug.

"Thank you. I made reservations for seven. I'm ready when you are." Laura said.

The dogs sauntered into the living room wagging their tails. "Hey, guys. How are you doing?" Marc pet each of the Siberian Huskies on their foreheads. They licked his hand in a sign of affection.

"I'll just take a few minutes, then we'll go." He said to his fiancee. Marc walked over to the bathroom. He observed the bedroom door was closed, as usual, when the dogs were inside. He knew Laura kept her cats and dogs separated and was amazed at how these animals were able to keep their distance in a small casita. He knew Laura cared about them. Laura had told him that her ex-husband didn't want the pets, so she took them after their divorce.

Marc splashed cold water on his face and changed his shirt. He took out his toothbrush and put it next to Laura's. He felt glad to be here and didn't want to think about work. He put on his suede blazer and took Laura's hand. "I don't know about you, but I'm hungry. Ready?"

"Yes, agent. I'm ready." Laura smiled and locked up the casita.

As they drove to Water Street, they observed the people walking along Alameda. The Indian Market brought people from all over the world and it was dinner time. For a split second, Agent Bennett wondered what the people on the grassy hill behind the Cross were doing. Then, Marc looked along the Santa Fe River. Chief Romero said the homeless find places to hide there, too. He looked at Laura.

Laura caught his eye. "It's so good to see you, Marc." She smiled and he reached for her hand.

They arrived in the large parking lot behind the Piano Bar. Marc got out first and opened the passenger door. He took her hand and helped Laura step out. They heard live music as they approached the large entrance door. It was a full house on this Saturday night.

Laura recognized the song being played. "This is a George Gershwin tune, Rhapsody in Blue. I read that the pianist is a graduate of the Julliard Music School in New York. He's very popular in Santa Fe."

The hostess approached them at the door and Marc said "Reservations for Bennett."

"It will be a few minutes. Would you like a seat at the bar?"

"That would be fine." They found two seats at the long Mahogany bar. Marc motioned to the bartender. "Laura, what will you have?"

"Red wine for me." She responded.

"I'll have a seltzer water with lime." Said Marc.

"There's so much talent here in Santa Fe. Marc, let's make a request. Do you want to hear something special?" Laura asked.

"Well, I like Burt Bacharach's music." Their drinks came. Marc paid the bartender then made a request for the music. He gave the bartender a ten-dollar bill. The bartender walked over to the piano. He put the ten dollars in a tip jar and said something to the pianist.

"We have a request to hear something from one of my favorite American composers, Burt Bacharach. This is for Marc and Laura." The pianist announced.

Marc nodded to the pianist and raised his glass. "I've just learned something new about you." Laura said.

"What's that?" he asked.

"Now I know your favorite music. I'll be sure to get some recordings to keep at the house."

They enjoyed the music awhile before the hostess arrived to escort them to their table in the dining room. The restaurant was designed so that dinner guests could still hear the live music in the background while having dinner.

The waiter approached and looked at Marc. "I haven't eaten since this morning, so I'm having Surf and Turf."

The waiter looked at Laura. "I'll have broiled salmon and broccoli."

Marc leaned back in his chair and looked at Laura. "It's been over a year since we met, but it seems like yesterday."

"Yes, the year has flown by. I walked by the gallery this morning. It's still closed. I thought it was up for sale after the owner was arrested." Laura said.

"It's up for sale. It's in an expensive area, so I guess it takes a special buyer." Marc replied.

"Yes, there is a stigma attached to it, too. A prospective buyer may not want that history attached to the building. Well, not our problem anymore." Laura sipped her wine and felt the round pendant on her neck, the Cherokee Star. She had a tendency to hold the pendant when she thought of that unpleasant experience.

Marc changed the subject. "How's school going so far?"

"My second graders are immature having just returned

from summer break. They need help learning the routine. They look forward to recess, that's for sure!" Laura laughed.

The waiter brought their meals. Laura ordered another wine and Marc another seltzer water. They enjoyed their meals while listening to the songs in the other room.

Marc took a break from eating. "The Chief told me you discovered the victim's binder today. It helped to identify him by the photo on his resume. That was very observant of you."

"Well, I guess I'm just a sleuth at heart. I thought there might be a connection to the empty display booth." Laura said modestly.

Laura looked around the dining room. "I love this room with the tall ceilings, large windows, and Saltillo tile floors. Look at the wood trim and plaster walls. It's so elegant. It's so Santa Fe."

"Yes, I agree. Speaking of rooms, we have to discuss where we will live when we get married. Albuquerque or Santa Fe?" Marc asked.

"I know, I've considered that. Maybe we can look around the southern part of Santa Fe, closer to Interstate 25? New developments are being built in that part of the city. That way, I can still teach here and you would have easy access to the Interstate." Laura explained.

"That's a good idea. Let's take a drive around town after breakfast tomorrow." Marc paid the check and they left the boisterous Piano Bar.

"I'm taking a short detour, Laura." It was dark outside and streets were quiet with only a few pedestrians near the Plaza. Marc turned onto the Paseo and proceeded past the Cross of the Martyrs on the hill overlooking downtown. He spotted a patrol car parked along a side street.

"Laura, I discovered there are campers up there behind the Cross."

"Campers so close to downtown?" Laura asked.

"Yes. I told the Chief to station a patrol car nearby. Be aware of your surroundings, Laura."

"I always bring pepper spray when out walking. Do you have any leads on your suspect?" she asked.

"Based on what the victim told witnesses, he saw someone acting like he was on drugs. The victim thought the guy was having a bad experience in town before the Market opened. It's our only guess, so far." Marc explained.

"Let's go home, Marc." They drove in silence to Pena Court.

Before leaving his vehicle, the agent retrieved his badge and firearm. He took them inside the casita and put them in the desk drawer.

He wanted to be with his fiancee and forget about solving crimes for the night.

CHAPTER 8

Laura slept in while Marc quietly slipped out for coffee. He grabbed his firearm and badge from the desk drawer and secured it in his vehicle. The coffee shop on Garcia Street was close by, so he went there. At eight a.m. tables were already filling with early risers. Marc ordered an Americano and bought the Sunday Santa Fe Journal.

He sat down at a table and glanced at headlines. At the bottom of the front page, he noticed a headline.

Murder at Indian Market. *A young Hopi Indian man was murdered early Saturday morning in the lot across from the Convention Center. Police aren't releasing the name of the deceased, but say he was an artist at the Market. There are no motives or suspects at this time. If you have any information,* *please contact the Santa Fe Police.*

Marc wanted to continue his search for the suspect. He, also, wanted to spend some time with Laura. He turned to the Real Estate section of the paper and looked at the Sunday Open House schedule. There were a few homes open in the south part of the city. He would suggest they visit today.

The agent ordered two coffees to go and got into his Jeep. He drove over to the Paseo towards the Cross. He saw a patrol car parked nearby. He got out of his vehicle and showed his badge to the officer on duty.

"Good morning, officer. I'm Marc Bennett with the FBI, here to assist in the murder of the artist yesterday. Did you see any suspicious activity?"

"I got here at 5:30 a.m. and saw some people up by the Cross. No one came down from that direction yet." Replied the officer.

"With the crowds here again today, the suspect may come back to panhandle the crowd. You have his description, right?" The officer nodded. Marc continued. "If you see him, take him in for questioning. Here's my card. Call me if you pick anyone up." Marc returned to his car and drove back to Pena Court, scanning the side streets as he drove.

Laura was up and the dogs were wagging their tails when Marc entered.

"Good morning, sweetheart. I didn't want to wake you, so I went for coffee. Here's one for you." Marc handed her the cup. He set the paper down and pointed to an article. *Murder at Indian Market.* "The news was bound to get out with the police presence in town."

"Well, people should be aware there's a murderer on the loose. "Laura said.

"Hey, I thought we could look at some open houses while I'm here. I noticed 3 or 4 places we can visit between 11 and 1 p.m. That still gives me time to work." Marc explained.

Laura smiled. "That's sounds great! I'll take the dogs for a walk and when I return, we can go to our favorite restaurant for breakfast. I'd like to stroll the Market awhile, too. By then, the home tour should be open."

"I'll check in with the Chief while you're gone." Marc sat in the armchair Laura's uncle made for her. It was a wedding present and she kept it after the divorce.

"Good morning, Chief. Agent Bennett here. Any activity since last night?" Marc asked.

"Hello agent. Well, I contacted the Director of the Homeless Shelter about some of the people I sent there recently. The Director said two people, a man and a woman, were trying to get straight and turn their lives around. They came in separately. They're both doing volunteer work at the Shelter. I'm going over there today at 3 p.m. to meet them. I want to speak to them about being informants in the homeless camp on the hill. It's a longshot, but it might help solve the case." The Chief explained

"I can join you at 3. I'll meet you at the station. I haven't heard from the relatives, so I'll call the Hopi Tribal Police again. There's another Hopi artist at the Market who knew the victim well. She was in shock yesterday, so I'll re-visit her today." Marc said.

"Another thing, agent. I asked Garland to send up more FBI agents today. We have a small force here and we need more eyes on the street. They are to check in here at the downtown Station and should be arriving soon."

"Glad to hear it, Chief." Marc hung up and heard the door open. Laura and the dogs had returned.

"I've got to make one more call before we go." Marc told Laura. He went outside on the patio for privacy. He dialed the Hopi Reservation. "This is Agent Bennett, with the FBI. Is your Chief available to speak to me?"

The officer responded. "The Chief is not in today, but I can call him and give him your number."

Marc gave his cell number and waited a few minutes. He looked up at the cloudless sky. It would be another warm day in Santa Fe. His phone rang. "This is agent Bennett."

"Agent Bennett, I was going to call you about the deceased. I visited his mother and sister last night. They were in mourning. I asked his sister, Lois, if she had spoken to him after he arrived in Santa Fe. She said Raymond called her Friday night. He said he would just sleep in his van since it was across from the Convention Center downtown. While they were talking, she heard a loud clammer on the other end. Her brother was yelling at someone. When he got back on the phone, she asked what the noise was. He said there was a man pounding on the window asking for money. Raymond yelled at the man to go away."

"Did Lois ask for a description of the man, by any chance?" Marc asked.

The Chief replied. "She asked her brother if he felt safe to stay there and he said he didn't want to leave his bronzes alone in the van. He told her the guy was Anglo and looked messed up, maybe on drugs. He said he would call her back after the Market on Saturday. That's it."

"OK, thanks. We've got eyes on the street and may put someone undercover in the homeless camp near downtown. The local police told me sometimes the campers take drugs and wander into the downtown area. That's the angle we're looking at right now. I'll keep you informed."

Marc went inside. "I'm ready if you are." He saw Laura filling the dog bowls. She grabbed her purse and hat and they went to the Jeep. "I'm meeting Chief Romero at 3. Let's go get some Huevos Rancheros. I'm hungry."

Downtown parking was scarce, so they walked four blocks to the restaurant on San Francisco Street. It was 8:30 a.m. and there was a short line to be seated. In the hotel lobby, Laura noticed an artist in a chair sketching someone.

Soon, they were escorted into the colorful restaurant.

Though it was daytime and the tall ceiling had skylights, strands of white lights were strung across the room. As they were being escorted to their table, Laura heard different languages being spoken. Along with English, people spoke German, French, Italian and of course, Spanish.

"Are you having your usual, Marc?" Laura asked. She already knew the answer.

"Yes, I am. Huevos Rancheros with green chile. And you?"

"Me, too. We have great taste!" She smiled and looked around the room. "There's such a diverse group of people here. It's so exciting! You know, I read that there's a special mass at the Cathedral today to celebrate Indian heritage. There will be a drum circle and singers at the entrance. Corn maidens will spread pollen on the church floors before the priests and Native Elders enter. It should be quite a celebration of faith and culture. Maybe we can go?"

Their plates arrived. "We'll see. It depends on the time of the mass." Marc stated. They ate their breakfast and commented on the great flavors of Southwestern cuisine. When finished, Marc ordered two pastries to go. He paid the bill. When Laura was ready, they visited the concierge at the hotel.

"Excuse me. Do you know when the mass at the Cathedral starts this afternoon?" Laura asked.

The man looked up from his counter and replied. "Yes,

that starts at three. It gets crowded, so I'd get there early if I were you."

Laura thanked the man. "Marc, if you're meeting Chief Romero, I can go to the mass. Perfect timing!" They strolled the hallway of the hotel and saw a sculpture of the famous *Zozobra* behind a glass case. Nearby, they saw a framed painting of a Buffalo Dancer. Laura visited the restroom and Marc sat in front of a fireplace with a large bas relief of Kachina figures.

Laura returned and looked at the relief mounted on the fireplace. "This hotel is loaded with history and art. Tourists must really enjoy staying here. "

Marc rose from his seat. "Well, I certainly enjoy the food! Let's go." Marc took Laura's hand as they left the dark hotel lobby and went out into the bright sunlight. The streets were crowded.

Marc scanned the faces around him while Laura looked at the artwork. They walked down San Francisco Street to Lincoln, then over to Palace Avenue. Marc saw the Food Truck he visited yesterday. While Laura was at a nearby booth, Marc visited the owner again. "Excuse, me. I spoke to you yesterday about the Hopi artist. Did you see anything unusual today?"

"I remember you. FBI, right? Actually, I did see a guy early this morning. Long brown hair. He had a blank stare as he walked down Palace Ave. He looked like he was on drugs, or off drugs for some mental condition."

"What time was that?" Marc asked.

"Maybe 7:30. I was making coffee. Streets were near empty, but I noticed him. He was Anglo, maybe six feet. In his 20's."

"You're Ben, right?" Marc asked.

"Yea, Ben Roybal."

"Do you have a phone in there, Ben?"

"I just got a cell phone Friday." Ben replied.

"If you see that man again, anytime of the day or night, call police. Describe where he was last seen. OK, Ben?" Marc insisted.

"Yes, sir. Got it!" replied the Food truck owner.

Marc found Laura and they turned right on Sheridan and walked over to Marcy Street. Laura was smiling. "There's so much creativity and beauty here."

"Yes, and I have a murder case to solve around all this beauty. Let's go visit the Hopi artist I met yesterday. She knew the victim." They found the booth with the artist's name, *Evelyn*.

Laura's eyes widened in delight. "Oh, this is the bronze I admired. The Harmonious One, right?"

"Hello again. Yes, she's the Harmonious One." Said the artist.

Laura couldn't take her eyes off the sculpture of the serene woman. "Isn't she lovely, Marc?"

Marc smiled at the artist. "Hello again, Evelyn. Did you think of anything since we spoke?"

"I tried to think of anything unusual. Last time I saw Raymond was at the Convention Center Friday morning. He had set up his entry piece and suggested we all meet for dinner Saturday night. That's all." Evelyn explained.

"Anything else, Evelyn?" Marc asked.

"I called his sister last night. She was very sad. She said she heard Raymond yelling at someone outside his van while she was on the phone with him. When it quieted down, he said it was some crazy Anglo demanding money. Maybe that's who killed him?" Evelyn asked.

"Yes, that's possible. We've gotten the same description from other people who saw a man acting strangely around the Market." Marc replied.

Evelyn reflected a moment. "Raymond and I were blazing a trail for the Hopi tribe with our sculpture. Hopis are known for basketry, pottery and Kachinas, not sculpture. It's a big financial investment to make a bronze and there are very few foundries in Arizona. Raymond was really making a name for himself and his clan. He was a sweet soul. The first bronze he made was a small owl. He called it his guardian spirit. He had it mounted on his dashboard. I miss him already."

Laura approached the Hopi artist and put her arm around her shoulder. "I'm so sorry for your loss, Evelyn. You are so talented. I hope you continue creating art. Keep blazing that trail in your friend's honor."

Evelyn wiped tears from her cheeks. "Yes. He would want that."

"Evelyn, tell Lois to call me to make arrangements for her brother's remains and possessions." Marc said goodbye and walked away. He waited for Laura.

"I love your work, Evelyn. Do you take payments?" Laura asked the artist discreetly.

"I do take payments for larger works. Here's my card. I'll be here until noon Monday."

"Wow! A lay away plan for art. What great news! I'm going to think about it. I just love this sculpture. I feel like she's alive, just sitting in harmony in her surroundings."

"Laura, you have understood the essence of my creation. You are very intuitive."

The women shook hands and Laura joined Marc. They walked to booth #35. The yellow crime tape was still around the booth.

"I'm going to talk to some of the nearby artists. Then we can go to the Open Houses."

Laura replied. "OK. I'll get some fry bread and see you back here."

Marc took out his badge as he approached the booths. "Did you see a man acting strangely this morning? Did you see anything suspicious earlier today?"

A man with wooden sculptures remembered something.

"Yes. I was here at about 7:30 setting up. I saw a young man with long hair looking in the trash cans. He looked dirty, like he slept in his clothes. He had a mean look on his face. He was white. Tall, maybe 6 feet and skinny. He wore black pants and a white tee shirt. I couldn't leave the booth and didn't see Security until later."

"Where was he headed?" Marc asked.

"He went down Marcy St., then turned left on Washington."

Marc got the man's name and number. "Thank you, sir. Be sure to call police if you see him. Don't approach him!"

CHAPTER 9

Marc scanned the faces in the crowd. Despite the news in the Sunday paper, the streets were thick with visitors at the Market. Marc noticed more of a police presence than the previous day. On East Alameda, he recognized someone, a fellow agent. "Hey, Jim, it's good to see you here." The two men shook hands. Marc introduced Laura to Jim.

"So, Marc, do you have any solid leads on a suspect yet?" Jim asked.

Marc explained. "There have been witness sightings of a younger white man with long brown hair, black pants and white tee-shirt acting strangely around town. He's been seen often in the early morning. Witnesses describe him as being on drugs or having a mental disorder. He may be homeless. Chief Romero said the warm weather brings more transients to town. Some camp in the hillside and along the river."

"I noticed some young people panhandling on the less crowded streets. Some of them were demanding cash and harassing people. I told them to move along and leave the visitors alone." Jim stated.

"Call for back-up if anyone needs to be picked up for disorderly conduct. This Indian Market is the biggest event of the year for these artists and they should be able to feel safe." Marc said good bye to his fellow agent, then he and Laura returned to the car.

Marc opened the passenger door. "Laura, when you're walking around town, be cautious."

"I know. I usually bring pepper spray with me. I didn't bring it today, since I'm with you."

They drove onto the Paseo and head out of the downtown area. Laura looked at the newspaper's real estate section. "There's a townhome just off Rodeo Road. Two bedrooms, one and a half baths, enclosed yard, two-car garage in our price range." They found the home. The Realtor greeted them and gave them a flier with information. After roaming the property, they both agreed it was too small. They needed a larger yard and would prefer another bedroom and bath.

"There's a home on Richards Avenue, near the college campus. Three bedrooms, 2 baths, large yard. More expensive than we discussed, but let's look." Laura said. As they drove, Marc recalled coming this way to interview Joyce Jordan's roommate at IAIA. The victim's body was found in the nearby grassy area. He noticed Laura holding her pendant around her neck. When she thought of Joyce Two Feathers Jordan, Laura held the Cherokee Star.

They found the open house and took a look around. "This is nicely updated." Laura commented. "Let's see the yard." They went outside and saw a large yard surrounded by the traditional wooden fencing found in the Southwest. Called coyote fencing, it consisted of tall cedar posts tied together by wire.

Marc approached. "What do you think?" he asked.

"I like it. There's enough room for all of us." Laura replied.

"Can I answer any questions?" The Realtor asked.

"How close to 1-25 are we?" asked Marc.

"You're about ten minutes out." The Realtor replied.

"That's good. I work in Albuquerque, so I want quick access to the Interstate." The visitors took the Realtor's card and decided to drive around the area.

Back in the car, Laura said there was one more house to visit. "There's a place in La Cienega, just south of Santa Fe. It's on an acre. Do we have time to visit?"

Marc looked at his watch. It was 1:30. "Yes, we can make it. Let's go." Laura gave him directions and they found a historic-looking pueblo style home with a fenced area. They saw the open house sign and went inside.

The Realtor greeted them. "Welcome. This is a three bedroom, two bath home on one acre of land. It is on city water. Some homes have their own well, but this has city water. Please look around."

Marc and Laura quickly visited each room, noticing areas that may need updating. They proceeded to the yard. It was nicely landscaped with a patio under the portal. The fencing was the traditional coyote fence. Marc approached the Realtor. "What are the boundaries of the property?"

They went outside to the front of the house and walked the lot. "We will take your information and contact you if we want to return. This is something to consider." Marc said. They got in the car and drove north.

"I'll time how long it takes to get to the Interstate, and the time it takes to get to Rodeo Road from here." Laura said. "This is a small village, but it's closer to Albuquerque for you and it has more land than we could get in Santa Fe."

"Yes, I'm glad we came here today. Now we have a better idea of what we can get for the money. "Marc replied as he drove back to the downtown area.

CHAPTER 10

Chief Romero sat at his desk this Sunday afternoon eating the Indian Taco his Lieutenant bought for him at one of the Market's Food Trucks. It was a tasty treat and hard to find around town the rest of the year. It was a long weekend, so the Chief savored his quiet time to enjoy a meal.

He took his pen and paper to write down questions he would ask the people at the Shelter today. He needed to be sure his informants wouldn't take drugs if offered. He decided to call the Shelter Director. "Ms. Garcia, before I visit the Shelter today, do you know what I can offer these people to get them to assist?"

"Well, Chief, Jerry Montano wants a job. He used to

work construction. Susie Jones enjoys serving meals here, so getting a job at a restaurant might be an incentive."

"OK, I can work that angle. Can they stay at the Shelter while working on the outside?" The Chief asked.

"Yes. We can keep them up to sixty days, then they move on. There's transition housing on West Alameda. They will need a bicycle or public transportation to their jobs. I have found that if they are motivated to stay clean, they'll do what it takes." Explained Director Garcia.

"This is good to know before I talk to them. I may bring an FBI agent who's working the case with me. He wants to meet the potential informants." The Chief hung up and looked at police reports for the past three days in Santa Fe.

The murder was Saturday morning. Since then, there were two calls for domestic violence, three calls for retail theft, one car break-in in a public lot, and four calls for disorderly conduct. He called in his Lieutenant.

"Tell me about these disorderly conduct reports." The Chief instructed.

"Sir, a Food Truck owner and three artists selling at the Market called to report a man acting erratically, as if he were on drugs. He went around the Market demanding money."

"What's the description?" Asked Chief Romero.

The Lieutenant read the reports in detail. "Tall white man, maybe 25-30 years old, long brown hair. They said he looked agitated and was aggressive. By the time an officer arrived at each location, the man was gone."

"OK, we have to find this guy! Put out a BOLO. Send a sketch artist to meet with each of the callers. I think this is our suspect." The Chief insisted. He had a few hours before his meeting. Maybe the sketch would be done by then.

It was nearly 3 p.m. when Marc pulled into the downtown Police Station parking lot. He had dropped Laura off near the Cathedral and was now back to work. The FBI agent nodded to the officers at the desk and proceeded to the break room to refresh and get coffee. He then went to the Chief's office.

"Any updates, Chief?" Asked Marc.

"Yes, agent. We got four calls about disorderly conduct at the Indian Market all describing the same man. I sent a sketch artist out to meet with the callers. I just got a sketch back on my computer. Give me a minute." The Chief continued. "I'm sending the sketch to my department and to Agent Garland. A BOLO is out to find this guy."

Marc leaned in by the computer and took a photo with his phone's camera. He finished his coffee and the two men left the office in the Chief's official vehicle. They drove to the Homeless Shelter.

"We have to catch this guy, agent. Even if he's not the murder suspect, he's a danger to the community. This sketch will help."

"I agree, Chief. Let's get these informants out to assist."

The Shelter Director met the officers at the front hall

entrance. They introduced one another. "Welcome, officers. I have Jerry Montano and Susie Jones ready to meet you."

"Sir, I think we should interview them separately. We can switch after fifteen minutes. Then we can compare impressions." Marc suggested.

"I agree, agent."

Ms. Garcia escorted them to different rooms, a library and a medical office. The men sat behind a table and displayed their badges. Questions included: What kind of drugs did you do? What would you do if offered drugs? When you were homeless, where did you sleep? Do you think you can assist the police in going undercover? If you could have a job, what would you like to do? Do you think you can blend in with the homeless enough to ask some questions? They were shown the sketch of the man they needed to find.

Jerry and Susie switched interviewers. Jerry wanted a construction job and Susie wanted to work at a local restaurant. They both insisted they wanted to be clean and start new lives. The Chief told them to wait in the library while they discussed amongst themselves.

The Chief began. "What do you think, agent?"

"I think they can do it. They both seem motivated to stay out of trouble and off the streets. Jerry said the man in the sketch looked familiar. Susie wasn't sure. We could give them each a burner phone with the sketch of the guy's face. The phones can have a direct line to our cell phones. Let's give them each a flashlight and pepper spray for protection."

"OK, let's get them out there. I'll get some phones and supplies and meet you back here in an hour." The Chief stood to leave. "I'll tell Director Garcia they will be working with us."

Marc returned to the library to give more details to the informants. "OK, Jerry and Susie, this is your chance to help your community and help yourselves in the process. The suspect may camp in the hills, so we'll take you there. We're going to give you phones that link directly to ours. The phones will have an artist's sketch of the man you're looking for. You can call or text if you see him. Take a back-pack and a blanket to pretend you are homeless. If someone recognizes you, say you were arrested or hitch-hiked out of state. You can act as a couple or as total strangers. You decide. You'll probably be offered drugs, so be ready. Don't be tempted or it will impair your judgement. Don't take that chance."

Marc continued. "Listen to what others are saying. Tell people you've been gone and want to know what's been happening. Somebody might know something. Also, if you see the suspect, don't engage. Text us his location and leave the area."

"What if he's onto us?" Susie asked.

"If he suspects you're working with us, get away. We'll have police parked behind the hill and on the street below the Cross. I need to take your photos to share with officers, so they will recognize you." Marc positioned each of the informants against the wall and took their photos.

"Whatever you do, don't lose your phones and don't share them with anyone." Marc insisted.

Susie was looking nervous. She was biting her nails. "I'm getting scared."

Jerry looked at her. "You can do this. You're brave. I know you are."

Marc tried to assure them. "Look, just try to blend in with other campers. Look and listen. Be discreet when using your phones. Someone may try to steal it from you. Get each other's numbers in case you get separated." The agent smiled. "Try to relax."

Marc noticed Susie stopped biting her nails and was taking deep breaths. "Once you notify police of the suspect's location, leave the area and let law enforcement take over."

Jerry looked at Susie and said "OK, agent. We're ready."

"I'll wait here while you get your back-packs and a change of clothes. Don't tell anyone where you're going. Just that you have to leave." The informants left the room and Marc texted the Chief with their photos.

It was nearly four p.m. now. The Cathedral Mass would be ended. Marc texted Laura. "Busy until 5 or 6. Do you want to wait for me in the Plaza?"

A few minutes passed and a text arrived. "I'll be at the Plaza at five."

The Chief returned to the Shelter with two burner phones. "I got your text with the photos of our informants. I sent them out to the officers to be aware. I have officers taking the night shift to be parked near the Paseo and near the parking lot to the walking trails behind the Cross. Another shift starts at 5:30 a.m. The suspect has been seen in the early morning, so let's see if he comes out. I've got the cell phones on speed dial and 911."

"These young people are at-risk while they're out there, so let's hope this doesn't take long." Marc said.

The Chief replied. "I'll try to help them out when this is over, so they can both get on with their lives."

The informants came into the library with their backpacks. They were each given a phone before getting into the Chief's vehicle along with Agent Bennett. The four rode together in silence to the parking lot by the walking trails.

Before exiting the vehicle Marc spoke to the informants. "Don't make any other calls than to the police. Guard your phones. That's your lifeline."

CHAPTER 11

The Mass was over and Laura stood in awe outside the Cathedral as she watched the American Indians exit to the pounding of the drum and the sound of the singers. The Mass had been a celebration of Indian heritage and the Catholic faith. Laura knew she would always remember this. Having been raised in the Catholic tradition, she had never witnessed such a ceremony before.

When the priests and the Elders came out, they stood together around the drum circle. When the drumming stopped, the priests and Elders shook hands and went their separate ways. The crowd slowly dispersed from the Cathedral steps and Laura decided to go to the park adjacent to the Cathedral. She wanted some quiet time before walking to the Plaza. After such a spiritually moving event, she just wanted to sit quietly. She found a bench towards the back of the park and away from the streets. She brushed the leaves away and sat down.

She looked at her phone. The time was 4 p.m. She had another hour before meeting Marc. She put the phone in her purse and closed her eyes. She took a few deep breaths. She listened to the birds in the trees and heard distant voices from passers-by on the street. She heard a rustling in the bushes behind her, thinking it was a squirrel.

Laura felt something on her hair. More pressure, now. A hand? Someone was playing with her hair! She opened her eyes and saw a man standing in front of her. He was disheveled and had leaves stuck to his pants. Was he in the bushes? She turned around to see a woman playing with her hair. Laura tried to get up, but was blocked by the man. She reached into her purse for her pepper spray. It wasn't there. She didn't take it today, since she came with Marc.

"What do you want?" She asked as she held onto her purse.

"That's a nice purse you have there, lady. I'll bet you have some money in it." The man smiled and showed his crooked brown teeth. The woman was now starting to pull on Laura's hair.

Laura looked around for help, but there was no one close by. "I don't have any money, just my ID."

"Oh, I doubt that. Let me see what you have there." The man grabbed for the purse. Laura tried to get away, but the woman was holding onto her hair and the man was blocking her.

Laura tried to wrestle the bag away from the man, but he was too strong. She decided to let go of the purse and run. As she pulled her head away from the woman, Laura felt hair being pulled out from her scalp. The woman came after her, but Laura managed to run towards the street.

She got to Cathedral Place and looked for Security. No one. She took Palace Avenue over to the Plaza and found an officer. "Officer, I was just robbed over in Cathedral Park. A man and a woman took my purse. They were hiding in the bushes and took me by surprise."

The officer radioed his station and said he was in pursuit of a suspect in Cathedral Park. He told Laura to stay in the Plaza and he would return to file a police report.

Laura found a bench with an older couple and she sat beside them. Something was going on that caught her attention. On the stage, there were American Indians taking turns at the microphone. "Say their names! Don't forget them! "Laura saw signs that read *Murdered and Missing Indigenous Peoples.* People were marching around the Plaza. Some were holding photos of their missing or murdered relatives. Some people took photos of the marchers and a woman, maybe a reporter, was interviewing someone holding a photo. Laura was saddened at the thought of all these missing relatives and thought that having this march during Indian Market was a good idea.

She rubbed her head, feeling the area where her hair was pulled. She took some deep breaths and felt grateful she wasn't seriously hurt.

Within fifteen minutes the officer returned. He found the purse, but it was empty. He didn't see anyone in the park after searching the bushes and the grounds. Laura filled out the police report for a stolen cell phone, ID and keys.

"Officer, can you do me a favor and call Chief Romero? He's working with my fiance, Agent Bennett with the FBI. Maybe agent Bennett can come pick me up?" The officer radioed the Chief.

Marc got to the Plaza in ten minutes and found Laura. After thanking the officer, he asked her. "Are you alright? Are you hurt?" He checked her face for bruising.

"My head is sore from a woman pulling my hair, that's all. They have my keys, ID and my phone. I'll need to change my locks right away." Laura replied.

"I'll ask the Chief to send a patrol car to your casita until we get there to be sure no one breaks in." Marc gave Laura a big hug. "I'm glad you're OK. Do you feel like getting dinner? We can walk to a place nearby." Marc asked.

"Yes, I'd like that. Let's go to that place on Don Gaspar." They started walking arm in arm. "I don't feel safe knowing someone has my keys. How am I going to get to school tomorrow?" Laura worried.

"Maybe you can take the morning off? Don't worry. We'll figure this out." Marc explained.

As they walked down Don Gaspar's narrow street, a young woman approached them. She held out her hand and asked for money. It was a different woman than the one who attacked Laura. "Can you spare some money? I really need it." The girl said.

Laura moved closer to Marc and away from the girl. "Wait a minute." He said as he took out his phone. Marc pulled up the sketch of the murder suspect. He showed it to the girl. "Do you know this man?"

The girl squinted at the picture and shook her head. "Yeh, I know that guy. He's crazy, man."

"Do you know his name?" Asked the agent.

"He goes by the name *Wings*. People call him that because he likes to flap his arms around. He talks to himself, flaps his arms and turns in circles." The girl replied.

"Do you know where I can find Wings?" Marc asked.

The girl angled her head to the side and asked. "What do I get if I tell you?"

Marc looked in his wallet and got a twenty-dollar bill. He held it up to the girl. "Where does Wings live? I need to find him."

"He's homeless, man. A lot of us are. He likes to camp up

by the Cross on the hill. He can get real mean, so people leave him alone. I don't know what his problem is. Like I said, he's crazy!" Marc handed the girl the bill and she left.

Marc dialed the Chief's number. "Chief, the suspect is called Wings. He camps up on the hill behind the Cross. A homeless girl just identified him from the sketch. Send a text to Jerry and Susie with the suspect's name. I'm with Laura and we're going to have dinner. I'll keep my phone on."

He took Laura's hand and they entered the restaurant. They found a quiet table in the corner. Laura went to freshen up and Marc ordered her some wine. When Laura returned, she smiled at Marc. "Thanks for ordering the wine." She held onto her pendant. "I'm glad they didn't take my pendant, too."

"Yes and I'm glad they didn't hurt you more seriously." Marc looked at the menu. "I haven't eaten here before. I'm going to get turkey and dressing. How about you?" Marc asked.

"I'll have the same." Laura replied.

They sipped their drinks and Marc asked. "How was the Mass?"

"Oh, it was lovely. It was so moving. It was like nothing I've ever seen or heard before. Many of the Pueblos were represented. The Mass concluded with a drum circle and singers outside. When the drumming stopped, the priests and Elders shook hands. I was so moved by the ceremony that I just wanted to sit quietly in the park and process it. I had my eyes closed. That's when the couple approached me. They had been hiding in the bushes behind me."

Marc reached for her hand. "It must have been very frightening. You're safe now. I'm glad you enjoyed the Mass."

CHAPTER 12

Jerry and Susie decided to pretend they were a couple. Susie was a little nervous about her role as a police informant, so Jerry suggested they stay together. They took their backpacks and walked up the hill behind the famous Cross of the Martyrs. It was early evening and it would be light for a couple more hours. As they approached the top, they saw young people sitting on the grass. Some were in small groups. There were tents and tarps set up in the woods.

As they walked, they said hello and nodded their heads in greeting. Someone recognized Jerry. "Hey man, where have you been? Haven't seen you in a while."

"I've been hitch-hiking around the state, man. I met up

with Susie here and we hit the road. Just got back and need a place to rest for the night. Is it OK if we stay here?" Jerry asked.

"No problem, man. It's cool with us. There might be a few people who think otherwise, so just lay low and chill." The man said.

The pair found a spot close to the woods, where they could see people coming and going. They set down a tarp and took out their sleeping bags. Though they weren't romantically involved, they had to pretend they were. They sat close together and held hands. "Let's be discreet and look around." Jerry said. Over the next hour, a few people came and went. Some went down the front path towards the Paseo. They decided to walk around the area before it got dark. They took out some granola bars and put them in their pockets. Phones were in another pocket.

As they neared the famous Cross, they saw a group of girls who looked emaciated. They were sun burned and parched. One girl looked at Susie. "Hey, girl. What's up? You got any food?"

Susie took out a granola bar and gave it to the girl who shared it with her friends. "Are you from around here?" Susie asked the girls.

"One of us is. She ran away from home and stays with us now. We came from Colorado." Another girl asked Susie. "How about you? Are you from here?"

"He's from here, but I'm from back East. We met on the streets and hit the road for a while. Hey, I heard there was some commotion at the Market Saturday. We saw police around the Plaza. Do you know what happened?" Susie asked nonchalantly.

After chewing her granola bar, one of the girls said. "Somebody had a bad drug trip. A guy who stays up here. He's a mean dude. The word is he hurt someone in town."

Jerry asked. "What does he look like in case we run into him? I want to stay out of his way, if you know what I mean."

"Yea, stay clear. He'll hit you if you look at him the wrong way. Heck, he may hit you just for being here!" The girls nodded their heads in agreement.

"Is he here now? How do we know who he is?" Susie asked.

"Oh, you'll know coz he'll be flapping his arms up and down while turning in circles. People call him Wings. He's Anglo. Tall with long brown hair. He sleeps on the ground, anywhere he can. He's always looking for drugs. Since you're new here, he may hit you up for some."

Susie reached into her pocket and took out another granola bar. She gave it to the girls. "We don't do drugs anymore, so don't have any."

"Well, good for you, but if Wings finds you, he may want something else." The girls giggled as they split the second granola bar.

The informants walked over to the pathway that leads to town from the hill. They over-looked the City of Holy Faith and saw visitors taking photos. Jerry said. "We have to be alert tonight. This guy Wings could come out of nowhere."

"Yes, I know. I'm anxious to get this over with." They looked around to be sure no one from the camp was nearby. Jerry took out his phone and sent a text to the Chief and agent Bennett. "Wings is known to stay here. Word is, he hurt someone in town Saturday."

Jerry put his phone away and hugged Susie. "You're brave. Remember that."

"Let's keep walking, Jerry. Maybe we'll find him." They walked back up to the Cross and past the group of girls. They strolled past others who were smoking pot or just talking to themselves. The couple walked in the woods amongst the tents, careful not to step on anyone curled up in the grass. They walked back to their spot and noticed their backpacks were opened and clothes were strewn around the area. "Jerry, someone went through our stuff!" Susie exclaimed.

They put the clothes back in their packs and sat on their sleeping bags. "This is why we have to keep our phones hidden at all times. Don't leave it out of your sight." Jerry said emphatically.

"Yes, I know." Susie agreed. Jerry took out a small flashlight from his backpack. Susie took the pepper spray out of her shirt pocket. The two informants sat in silence as night darkened the scene before them.

Further back in the woods, the man known as Wings was on the hunt for drugs. Now he had something to trade. He had a bronze owl, gas card and money. He walked around the tents, looking for someone he could trade with.

CHAPTER 13

Marc and Laura were finishing their meal. "I have to call the owner of the casita. He has to know my keys were stolen. Can I use your phone, Marc?"

Before handing the phone over, Marc checked for messages. He read a text from Jerry, the informant. He gave Laura the phone.

While Laura talked to her landlord, Marc paid the bill and thought of what he would do next.

"The owner is coming over to meet a locksmith early in the morning. I should be there to get the dogs out of their way. Then, I'll need a ride to the car dealership to get a spare key. If you're busy, I'll call a friend. I'll need to buy a new phone, too. It's a good thing I hid a spare house key outside."

Laura explained.

"We'll see how it goes. I'm taking you home now, then I'm going to park near the Plaza and look around. Since the Market is over, artists are packing up to leave. The suspect may come out to look for scraps."

They left the restaurant and walked to Marc's vehicle. They passed a group of young people with backpacks sitting by the city parking lot. They looked tired and messy. Marc decided to talk to them.

"Hey, guys, we're looking for someone. He left something behind at the restaurant and we want to give it back." Marc showed the group the sketch on his phone.

One man said "I don't know." Another took a closer look. "Yea, I've seen that dude around. He looks for stuff in the trash cans. If he gets excited, he flaps his arms up and down and turns around. He doesn't say much. I try to avoid him."

"Any idea where he might be?" Marc pushed for more information.

"I've seen him up by the Cross and once over by the river on Alameda." The man replied.

Marc took out his wallet. "Guys, get yourselves something to eat." He gave them a twenty-dollar bill.

"Thanks, man."

Marc and Laura got to the car and drove back to the casita. A squad was sitting in front as Marc had requested. Marc introduced himself and gave the officer his cell number.

"I'm dropping Laura off and I'm going back to work. Can you stay here until I return?" Marc asked.

"Yes, the Chief wants me to stay here. I'll be here unless someone else comes to relieve me."

"We really appreciate it, officer. I'm working the Indian Market murder case. With Laura's keys and ID stolen, I don't want her to be alone. She has two dogs and may bring them out for a walk. They'll stay nearby."

"Thank you, officer. "Laura said before she went inside the casita.

Marc made sure the casita was secure while Laura got the leashes for the dogs. He changed his shirt and shoes and put on a warmer jacket for the cool night ahead. He made sure he had his firearm, a radio, phone and zip ties.

"Stay in view of the officer when you're with the dogs. I'll be back later." Marc hugged Laura before leaving.

Laura went inside and leashed her dogs for their nightly walk. It would be shorter than usual, since she had to stay close to the squad car. She walked back and forth down the short dead end street. She was near the end of Pena Court when she heard voices nearby. She took a few more steps and looked around the corner to Acequia Madre. Laura squinted to see who was approaching on the street and gasped. It was the pair who robbed her!

Laura quickly turned around and dragged her dogs along as fast as she could. She went to the squad car and waved to the officer to roll down his window.

"Officer, the people who robbed me are coming this way! They probably want to see if they can break in."

"OK. Take the dogs down to the neighbor's driveway and wait there. I will move the vehicle behind the bushes and go wait for them. I'll call for back up." The officer instructed.

"Come on, guys. We're going to hide out for a while." Laura told her dogs as they moved down the street.

The officer hid his vehicle and got out. He turned his radio down and unstrapped his weapon as he approached the casita. He saw a scraggly-looking man and woman walk down Pena Court, closely looking at house numbers. The man looked at something in his hand and read the numbers to his partner. "Here it is. Let's go!" He said excitedly.

They walked through the iron gate and to the front door of the casita. He tried the keys. The door opened. "Bingo!" he exclaimed. The pair entered the front door and was followed by the police officer.

"Hold it right there!" the officer demanded.

The couple turned around in surprise and saw the officer with his weapon pointed at them. They put their hands up. "OK, OK. We're unarmed. Cool it, man." The robber said.

The officer turned up his radio and called. "I have two robbery suspects at this location. Request back-up."

"Stand against the wall with your hands behind your backs. Now!" The officer demanded.

He took out his zip ties and tied the man's hands first, then the woman's. "You're under arrest for robbery, assault and breaking and entering. You have the right to remain silent. Anything you say can and will be used against you in a court of law. You have the right to an attorney."

The officer felt the man's pockets and found a set of keys and an ID. The ID said *Laura Barnes*.

The pair was ordered to walk outside, where they were held until another squad arrived.

In the meantime, Laura slowly walked her dogs near the casita. She saw that the man and woman were apprehended. The dogs barked at the couple. "That's them! They robbed me earlier today." The man showed his brown teeth and the woman sneered at her.

"I have your ID here, Laura. They had your keys and ID." The officer handed Laura her items. The car key was still there.

"What did you do with my phone?" Laura asked the thieves.

"We got some money for it. It's long gone, lady." The woman said sarcastically.

A second squad car pulled up and a female officer got out to assess the scene. "Officer, please take this woman into custody. I'll meet you back at the Lincoln Avenue Station with this guy. They've been read their rights. There's no personal identification on them. They will have to be finger-printed and processed. This is the victim and witness." He pointed to Laura.

"I got back everything but my phone. I still want to press charges." Laura stated. "Can you call Agent Bennett and tell him you're leaving with the offenders? I appreciate your help with this matter."

The robbers were loaded into the squad cars and Laura went back inside the casita. She locked the doors behind her and fell on the couch. Her dogs lay down beside her as she closed her eyes and let out a long sigh of relief.

Since she didn't have a phone, Laura couldn't call Marc or the owner of the casita. She would just have to wait and try to unwind from the eventful day.

CHAPTER 14

A tall shadow came out of the woods and approached the couple. It was a man in a white tee shirt. He came towards the couple and got too close for comfort. Jerry turned on his flashlight.

"Hey, man. What's happening?" Jerry asked. He couldn't see the face, but could tell it was a man. A tall man.

Susie held onto her pepper spray and aimed it towards the man. She heard a grunt. Then, the word *drugs*.

"We don't have any drugs, man. We're clean. We just want to rest for the night." Jerry told the man.

The man turned in circles. "Drugs. Give me some drugs. Now!" he demanded.

Jerry shined the light up at the man's face. It resembled

the sketch. The man was angered at the light in his eyes and lunged down at the couple. He reached for the light, but Jerry moved away. Susie screamed and aimed the pepper spray at the man's face. He covered his eyes. Then he waved his arms up and down and screamed while turning in circles.

Jerry got up and pulled his companion off the ground. "Run!" Susie stumbled in the dark. Jerry picked up his backpack and threw it at the man. He ran after Susie.

Jerry looked behind him and saw the man following them. His balance was off, but the suspect stayed in pursuit.

"We've got to get to the police." Jerry said. "We're almost there. Come on!" They ran down the hill to the parking lot. It was dimly lit and empty. They spotted the squad car in the far corner.

As the informants neared the squad, they yelled. "Help! Help!" They waved to the officer who got out of the car.

"We're working with Chief Romero. The suspect, Wings, followed us down the hill." Jerry said.

"Get in the car and stay there." The officer radioed for back-up.

Jerry and Susie took out their phones and texted the Chief and agent Bennett. "Wings is on the back side of the hill. He followed us to the parking lot. We're in the squad car now."

The informants sat quietly as they watched the officer in front of them search the area. Within a few minutes, they heard a siren, then saw the flashing lights pull up next to them. Chief Romero got out of the vehicle. "Are you two all right?" He asked.

"Yes, we're fine, just shaken up. Wings lunged at us and followed us down here. He must be in the woods." Jerry explained.

"Stay in the car. I'll have someone take you back to the Shelter." The Chief said. He got on his radio. "Suspect seen in the woods behind the Cross, near the visitors' parking lot. Cover the Paseo in front of the Cross, too. Officers are needed to search the nearby woods. Suspect was pepper-sprayed and may be visually impaired to our advantage."

A half hour earlier, Agent Bennett had parked his vehicle on Otero Street, facing the Cross. He got out and walked along Marcy Street. Most businesses were closed now and few people were out. He walked past a business with a sign in the window *For Lease*. As he walked past, he saw cardboard piled high inside an entryway. He thought that was unusual in downtown Santa Fe.

He looked more closely in the entryway and saw a shoe. He called out. "Hello. Is anybody in there?"

He heard someone moaning. "Are you all right? Do you need help?" The agent asked.

"No. Go away! Go away!" Someone said in a man's voice.

The agent was about to start dismantling the cardboard to see if it was the suspect when his phone pinged. He got a text from the informants. He dialed the Chief. "I'm on my way to the parking lot."

"The suspect is in the area. We have to find him! Call Agent Garland to notify the other FBI agents that we're here. We need help searching these woods." Chief Romero insisted.

Marc dialed his office and asked for Agent-in-charge Garland. "Sir, the suspect was just spotted in the woods. The Chief wants you to call agents nearby to help with the search. We're searching around the Cross of the Martyrs and the parking lot behind it."

"Two agents returned to the field office after the Market closed, but there should be three more who stayed in Santa Fe. I'll reach out and give them the update." Agent Garland hung up and Marc went to his vehicle. He proceeded to drive to the parking lot behind the Cross. There were four squad cars with lights flashing. Marc parked behind them.

He saw Chief Romero giving orders to officers, who left in pairs to search the woods. "Chief, Agent Garland has three agents still in the area. Where do you want us?"

"There are campers in the hills and people sleeping in the woods. It's tough looking in the dark, but we have to track him. Show the sketch to people who may have seen him. We're not here to bust anyone for drugs. We're here to catch a murder suspect. Also, at some point, we have to get these informants out of here."

"Yes, sir. I can take the pair back to the Shelter."

Marc went to talk to the informants. "How are you two

doing? It must have been frightening for you."

Susie's knees were shaking as she folded her hands tight. "I was so scared! If I didn't have that pepper spray, I don't know what would have happened to us. He was so angry!"

"Did he say anything?" Marc asked.

"He didn't say much. He just said the word *drugs*. He demanded drugs. When I flashed the light at his face, he got really angry and lunged at us. After Susie sprayed him, we ran. He followed us, like a mean dog. He's wasted. He's a dangerous guy. I hope you find him." Jerry said.

"I'll get you back to the Shelter as soon as I can. I'm waiting for back-ups to arrive. Stay put." Agent Bennett instructed.

While waiting in the car, Jerry reflected on the experience. "I don't know about you, but after seeing that guy so messed up, I don't ever want to do drugs again. Ever!"

"I know." Susie said. "Seeing those girls on the hill so burned and hungry made me sad. We're lucky we were taken to the Shelter. We're lucky to survive that lifestyle. Some of those people in the hills may not make it."

"Well, the Police Chief said he would help us out so we'll see what happens. I don't ever want to live on the streets again. I want a better life." Jerry said.

"I want a clean life and a good life. I don't have to be rich. I just want a roof over my head, a job and food to eat." Susie said.

"That's it?" asked Jerry.

Susie looked at him. "And good friends."

Jerry smiled. "You got it."

CHAPTER 15

Though his eyes were burning, the man continued his pursuit of the couple. He neared the parking lot, then saw a light traverse the ground below his feet. He knew enough to avoid walking into the light, so he went to the side and back up the hill. He needed water and a fix. He would continue looking around the campsite.

There was a sleeping bag near a backpack on the ground. He lifted the sleeping bag and covered his head. He rubbed his burning eyes with it. He saw a group of girls and stumbled towards them. "Water. Water. Give me water." Said the man.

"Hey, man. Get lost. We only have half a bottle to share between us." One girl said.

The man threw off the sleeping bag and walked into the

circle. "Water." He spun in a circle and slowly raised his arms before falling onto the ground. "Give me water."

"Oh, that's Wings." Said one of the girls. "He's a druggie. Give him the water before he does something crazy."

The man called Wings was handed the bottle and poured it over his eyes. He saved one drop for his mouth. He reached for the sleeping bag and rubbed his eyes with it. The girls moved away from him, hoping to avoid any further contact.

The man lay still for a few minutes, then rose to the smell of marijuana in the air. He grabbed the sleeping bag. His eyes weren't so blurry now, as he began to walk in the direction of the sweet smell. It was coming from a campsite in the woods.

Though it was dark, he saw glowing lights inside some of the tents. Some people sat outside under the stars. The sweet smell wafted through the cool night air. He was getting closer. The scent was strong near one tent so he looked inside. Three people were sitting in a circle smoking.

Wings left the sleeping bag outside and stepped inside the tent. The people looked dismayed at his entrance. The man held out his hand and reached for the marijuana.

"Hey, man, we're just trying to have a conversation here. Do you mind?" Someone said.

"Give me weed." Insisted Wings. The group paused and stared at the intruder. Wings reached over the seated men and grabbed the weed from the smoker's hand. He inhaled a long breath of smoke, then left the tent. He heard the men complaining behind him, but he didn't care. He continued smoking and gathered the sleeping bag before walking away.

Soon, he would need to find food. He found a spot to sit under the stars and continued smoking. His eyes were not quite focused as he tried to look up at the starlit sky. He heard murmurs from inside the tents and heard the trees rustling in the wind. It was getting cool in this high mountain air. He put the sleeping bag over his shoulders.

Out of the corner of his eye, he saw lights moving on the ground below. He turned his head and saw shapes moving in the darkness behind the lights. The lights were traversing across the grass below and were moving closer up the hill. His mind was not sure if he was hallucinating again or if these were real moving lights. He decided to move away from the lights.

The man called Wings stood up and tried to regain his balance. Standing up and walking was hard. He was stoned. He wrapped the sleeping bag across his shoulders and head towards the Cross. He wobbled as he moved around the people sitting on the ground. He heard someone say "Hey, watch out, man."

"Hey, you just stepped on my hand!"

Wings was hungry. Fry bread was his last meal and that was many hours ago. Maybe that was yesterday or the day before? He couldn't remember. He decided to walk down the winding path into town and look for food. He shielded his eyes from the spotlights around the Cross as he began his descent. He bumped into a railing and stumbled before hitting another railing. He held onto the cold steel with both hands, trying not to fall. He was dizzy and heard voices.

Where are they coming from?

The spotlights dimmed as he slowly moved down the path. The entrance to the street was close now. He lifted his head and saw more lights moving around the grass. Was he hallucinating? There were shapes behind the lights. Men. Women. Uniforms. Wings tried to focus his eyes to see what was before him. A bright light shone in his eyes. He swayed back and forth and tried to shield his eyes with the sleeping bag.

"Stay right there!" A man's voice said. "Stay right there! Put your hands up!"

Wings felt confused and slowly turned around in circles. He dropped the sleeping bag and tried to get away. He crawled under the railing, but was met by a dark shape. He turned to go back up the path, but was met by another dark shape. He tried to focus on the letters in front of him. POLICE. He turned around to see more letters. FBI.

Wings swayed like a branch in the wind. He felt metal rings being bound to his wrists. Someone reached into his pocket and found a small bronze owl. In another pocket was a gas card and money. They were put in evidence bags. Another card was found, a library card.

"Is this your ID? Are you Keith Jones?" A man in uniform asked.

"Wings. I'm Wings. What's happening?" Wings was feeling he was on a bad trip.

Chief Romero heard the radio call. "Suspect detained near the entrance to the Cross on Paseo."

Agent Bennett heard the announcement on his radio as he walked through the group of people sitting around the Cross. The FBI agent joined the officers who surrounded the suspect. He stood in front of the suspect. He looked at the sketch on his phone and it matched the man he was looking at.

"You're under arrest for the murder of Raymond Sakitewa. You have the right to remain silent. Anything you say can and will be used against you in a court of law. You have the right to an attorney." Agent Bennett announced.

The man called Wings could barely raise his head. He was under the influence of marijuana and nothing seemed real. "I need food. Give me food."

Chief Romero arrived to see the suspect in custody. He looked at the sketch and it resembled the man in handcuffs. He spoke to the officer who was holding Wings. "Take this man to the downtown Station. Book him for murder and put him in a cell. We'll give him some time to sleep it off. We'll be back to question him."

CHAPTER 16

gent Bennett told the Chief. "I'll go get the informants and take them back to the Shelter."

"OK. Tell them to keep the phones and that I'll visit them later in the day Monday. I want to make some calls about employment before I talk to them." Responded Chief Romero. "Do you want to question the suspect, agent?"

"Yes, I do. I'll be back at the Station in an hour." The agent walked back to his vehicle.

Agent Bennett called his office. "Agent Garland, we have the suspect in custody. It was helpful having the other three agents here to assist. I'm going to interview the suspect tonight. I'll return Monday."

"Agent Bennett. Take the day off tomorrow. We'll see you

here Tuesday noon to file your report."

"Thanks, Sir. I could use a little extra time up here."

Agent Bennett drove to the parking lot behind the Cross. There were two squad cars sitting idle. He exited his vehicle and approached the car with the informants. "Officer, I'm here to take these informants back to the Shelter. Thanks for your help today."

"No problem, agent. We're glad you got your suspect and nobody else got hurt." Replied the officer.

Jerry and Susie got out of the squad car and into the agent's vehicle. "Do you have anything left on the hill you want to take back with you?" Asked Agent Bennett.

"Well, we lost our backpacks and some clothes, but I don't want to go back up there." Replied Susie. Jerry agreed.

"You both did a good job today. Chief Romero said you can keep the phones. They're burners, so you'll have to pay to keep them active. The Chief will visit you later on Monday to talk about finding employment."

They arrived at the Shelter and Agent Bennett walked in with the pair. He signed them in at the front desk. He asked if the Director was in and was told she was gone for the day.

"I wish you the best." The agent shook Jerry's hand and held Susie's hand in his. "Keep clean and you'll be fine."

"Yes, sir." Replied Susie. "We decided we don't ever want to be homeless or do drugs again."

CHAPTER 17

Back at the Police Station, Chief Romero splashed cold water on his face. There was a fresh pot of coffee and donuts to be had in the Break Room. He took one of each and sat at his desk.

He took out a fresh notepad and pen and thought of questions he would ask the murder suspect. Of course, there was a good chance the suspect would not say anything or say anything that made sense. He buzzed the front desk.

"Yes, Chief." The officer replied.

"Let's get the murder suspect something to eat. It's late, but maybe you can get him a burger and fries or a sandwich. It may help his state of mind."

"Yes, Sir. I'll have another officer cover the desk while I go out." Replied the officer.

Based on the witness descriptions of the suspect's actions, the Chief knew he would need assistance from a Forensic Psychiatrist. He looked through his list of experts and found two names he had worked with in the past. He would see if either one was available tonight or first thing in the morning. After a few sips of coffee, he dialed the numbers.

One was out of town. The other could come in the morning. In the meantime, the Chief and Agent Marc Bennett would try to assess the suspect and get more information.

There was a knock on the door. "Agent, there's fresh coffee and donuts in the Break Room. Help yourself and meet back here." Instructed the Chief.

After cleaning up, the agent got coffee and a snack. He returned to the Chief's office.

"I'm getting the suspect something to eat. Who knows how long it's been since he ate. I realize he may not be talkative, but we can try to ask him some questions. I have a Forensic Psychiatrist coming to meet him in the morning. The Doctor can draw blood to see what drugs are in his system." The Chief continued. "We'll see how he does in the cell tonight."

"I understand. Let's see if we can get him to talk." The agent replied as he finished his donut.

The two men stood up and went to the Interrogation Room. Inside, they saw the man called Wings eating a hamburger and fries, still wearing hand-cuffs. The men entered the room and sat down across the table from Wings.

"I'm Santa Fe Police Chief Romero and this is Agent Bennett with the FBI. We want to ask you some questions."

Wings continued eating his food voraciously without acknowledging the men sitting across from him.

The Chief started. "Can you tell us your real name?" No response. "Are you Keith Jones?" The Chief showed the man the library card with the same name. No response.

"Are you from Santa Fe?" Agent Bennett asked. No response. "Did you come from another state?" No response.

"Do you have family we can call?" Asked the Chief. No response.

They waited for the man to finish eating. Once finished, they resumed questioning.

"Do you know you are being charged with murder? This man was killed in his van on Saturday morning." Agent Bennett took out his phone and showed Wings the photo of the victim.

Wings looked at the photo and shrugged his shoulders. He avoided making eye contact with the men. He looked around the room and stood up. He tried to raise his arms, but couldn't. He slowly started to rotate in a circle. The Chief called in an officer.

"Officer, tie the cuffs to the table so this man doesn't try to leave." The Chief instructed.

The officer approached the man rotating, but Wings got agitated. He resisted the officer and raised his arms to attack. The Chief got up and held one arm as the officer held the other. They moved the man to the table and attached the cuffs to the table.

"Stay here, officer." Said the Chief.

Agent Bennett showed Wings the photo of the victim again. "White van." Wings said.

"We found an owl in your possession, along with a gas card and money that was taken from the victim. The owl was mounted on the dashboard of the van. The white van. You took it after you killed this man." Explained Agent Bennett as he kept the photo open in the direction of the suspect.

"This man was a talented artist getting ready to sell his work at the Indian Market. You killed him." Bennett continued.

The man called Wings started pounding the table. He stomped his feet and shook his head. He avoided looking at the photo and avoided looking at the men seated across from him. He began pounding his head on the table.

The Chief stood and left the room. He called down the hall for assistance. Another officer arrived. "Take this man back to his cell. Make sure there are no sheets in the cell for him to hang himself." The Chief ordered.

The officers unlocked the cuffs from the table, then escorted Wings out of the room. Wings didn't resist this time.

His forehead was bruised from the pounding.

The men returned to the Chief's office. "Agent, this guy doesn't even know his real name. Let's hope his prints are in the system or we may never know. I'll check with the library to see if the name Keith Jones is in the system. There may be an address or phone number we can track."

"The drug use has impaired his mind, but he remembered the white van. The photo of the victim stirred his memory. I hope you can get the blood test done soon so we know what he's been taking. I'll be back in the morning. I'd like to know what the Psychiatrist thinks."

"Yes, Good night, Agent."

"Good night, Chief."

Marc went to his vehicle and dialed the number of the Hope Tribal Police. The agent identified himself. "Please tell Chief Shunpavy, there is a suspect in custody in Santa Fe. I will update him Monday with more information."

CHAPTER 18

Agent Marc Bennett went back to Pena Court. The lights were still on and the dogs greeted him when he entered. Laura was curled up on the couch watching the evening news.

"Good job, agent. The news said a suspect was in custody for the murder of the artist at Indian Market. They gave the victim's name and said he was from the Hopi Reservation in Arizona."

"The suspect fits the description from the witnesses. We found some of the victim's items in his possession, too." Agent Bennett took off his gear and unloaded his firearm. He put them in the desk drawer.

"Did he admit to anything?" Laura asked.

"When shown the victim's photo, he said *white van*. Somewhere deep in the crevices of his drugged-out mind, he remembered that."

"Well, I have some good news. My ID and keys were returned after the police caught the robbers trying to break in. I just have to get a new phone, now." Laura sat up on the couch as she explained. "I couldn't call the homeowner, so I'll just let him come as planned to change the locks for precaution."

"Do you want to call in for a personal day or half-day tomorrow? After your locks get changed, I can take you to get a new phone, then to school. I'm meeting the Chief late morning."

"Yes, I think a half-day is enough. Can I use your phone to call Principal Ramone?" Marc handed her the phone.

"I'm going to take a hot shower and wash off the dust. Then, I'm having a cold beer." The agent said as he unbuttoned his shirt.

Laura told her School Principal about the robbery and needing the morning off. Laura was told to take the whole day, since she just went through a traumatic event. This took some of the pressure off her. She turned off the television and dimmed the lights. She felt better now that Marc was back.

By seven a.m., the sun shone through the casita's windows and Laura's dogs were wagging their tails. Coffee was brewing and Laura got the leashes out. This would be a short walk since they would be going out again when the locksmith arrived.

She took her keys and pepper spray and closed the door quietly, so as not to awaken her guest. The locksmith and homeowner were coming at eight. She wanted to have breakfast ready by then.

Marc awakened slowly from a deep and restful sleep. He looked at his watch. It was 7:15. He smelled the aroma of coffee seeping under the door. He stood up to see a cat sitting on the window ledge. This room was the cat's domain and he respected her space. "Good morning, Gato." He greeted.

Marc put on a dress shirt and clean pair of jeans. He didn't plan to do much walking today, so wore boots instead of walking shoes.

He made himself a cup of coffee and checked his phone for messages. A text from Chief Romero. "Meet here at 11 a.m."

Laura returned with the dogs and greeted Marc with a hug. "Did you sleep well, agent?"

"Very well, thank you."

"I'll make us eggs, bacon and toast for breakfast. The locksmith will be here at 8." Laura said.

"Sounds good." The agent replied. He retrieved his gear from the desk drawer and stepped outside to load it securely in the back of his vehicle.

When he returned, breakfast was ready. They sat at the

small dining table. Marc saw a bowl of green chile next to his plate. He spooned some on his eggs. "This is great, Laura."

"You know what they say. Breakfast is the most important meal of the day!"

They had just finished their meals when they heard a knock on the door. The dogs barked. Laura saw the owner of the casita and let him in. Marc said his hellos from the kitchen, then told Laura he would be in his car making a call.

Laura explained to the owner that the keys were returned, but that as a precaution, she'd like the locks changed regardless. The owner agreed and she returned the old set of keys.

Laura leashed the dogs and left the casita just before the locksmith arrived. She waved to Marc in his vehicle, then proceeded to walk along Acequia Madre. The dogs enjoyed walking in the water, shallow as it was.

Laura walked over to Camino del Monte Sol and back to Pena Court. She stopped at Marc's vehicle. His window was rolled down and he was talking to someone. He held up his hand to indicate he needed to finish his call, so she walked the dogs a few minutes more. She returned to the parked vehicle.

After the call, he smiled at Laura. "Guess what?"

"Good news, agent?"

"That was Lois, the victim's sister. The Tribal Police Chief told her we caught the murder suspect. She wants to come to Santa Fe. Lois has to make arrangements to return her brother's body to Third Mesa and wants to retrieve his possessions."

The agent continued. "She said she got a call from the Indian Market Committee late Saturday morning. The art show judging was done Friday night and Raymond won first place in sculpture! Lois said her brother had a feeling he would win a prize this year. The judge was looking for Raymond at his booth early Saturday to give him his ribbon. Winners display their ribbons at their booths during the weekend to attract more collectors. Since no one was in the booth, the judge called the emergency contact listed on the entry form."

"Wow! That's great for his family legacy." Laura said.

"Lois said her brother dropped off his bronze entry at the Convention Center the day before. She needs to pick it up, along with the ribbon. Another thing the judge told her was that two collectors expressed interest in buying the winning bronze. Contact information was exchanged and Lois told the judge her family wanted to think about it." Marc explained. "I told Lois I would let her know when the victim's van and possessions can be released so she can plan her visit."

"That reminds me. I want to see Evelyn before she leaves. She said she's leaving her hotel at noon." Laura said.

They saw the locksmith get into his truck and Laura took the dogs back to the casita. She was handed her new keys and tried the locks. No problem. She thanked the homeowner and got the dogs back inside. She grabbed her purse with her ID, credit card, and pepper spray.

She entered Marc's vehicle. "Let's get you a new phone." Marc said as he drove away.

CHAPTER 19

They drove to Cordova Shopping Center and located the Phone Store. Marc waited in his vehicle while Laura shopped for a new phone. Marc called the Santa Fe Police Chief.

"Good morning, Chief. I'm coming in at 11 a.m. as requested. How's the suspect doing today?"

"I'm told he had periods of rest and agitation. He's mostly non-verbal, flails his arms and turns in circles. The Psychiatrist, Dr. Smithson, came early and drew some blood. The suspect needed to be held down by three officers."

"I'm glad that's done. Has he eaten anything today?" Asked the agent.

"He was given some fruit, toast and juice. I don't know if

he ate." Replied the Chief.

"When will you get bloodwork results?" The agent asked.

"Dr. Smithson will be back at 11 this morning with the results. We'll get more of an idea of his condition then."

"Good. I'll see you then, Chief."

Laura was returning to the car and was using her new phone. "I'll see you soon." She said. "Marc, I just spoke to Evelyn, the Hopi artist. I'd like to see her before she leaves. She's staying at the Hotel Santa Fe. Can you drop me off and we can meet up later?" Laura asked.

"Sure. I'd like to speak to Evelyn myself." Marc said as he drove towards Guadalupe Street.

Marc pulled into the parking lot of the Pueblo style hotel. Before entering, Laura stopped to look at the bronze sculptures. There was a life-sized warrior standing overhead on the ledge. There was the shape of a Buffalo Dancer on the wall. On a pedestal, sat an American Indian Chief in a War Bonnet with his arms stretched out and folded, as if in prayer. They strolled to the side of the entrance and saw another warrior with a sword in bronze mounted on a large rock.

"This is amazing! It's like being in a sculpture garden." Laura said excitedly.

"Yes, this is impressive. Let's go in. We may see more art inside." Marc took Laura's hand and they entered the Hotel. In the lobby, they saw Evelyn sitting in a chair.

"Hello agent. Hello Laura. Do you want to get something

to eat or drink? They have a great restaurant here." Suggested the artist.

Marc looked at his watch. It was 10:30.

"I'll sit with you for a few minutes, then I'll be leaving."

They proceeded into the part of the restaurant facing the patio where there was a large Teepee set up in one area and benches in another. The waiter arrived. Marc ordered orange juice and the ladies ordered coffee.

Marc began. "Evelyn, I heard from Raymond's sister, Lois, this morning. She said that her brother won a prize from the Market Committee. They had been looking for him at his booth and decided to call his emergency contact."

"That's great, agent. Raymond was hoping to win a prize this year."

"He sure did. He won first place in sculpture."

"Wow! Really?" Evelyn exclaimed. Tears started forming. "Oh, Raymond. He worked hard and was so looking forward to the Market. I'm happy for his family. When they need money, they can sell for a higher price now."

"Evelyn, when we talked earlier, you said Raymond had a bronze mounted on his dashboard. Do you know what that was?" Marc asked.

"Yes, it was an owl. That was the first bronze he made. He said it was his guardian spirit." Replied the artist.

"The reason I ask is that I noticed something was missing on the victim's dashboard. When the suspect was apprehended yesterday, the officers found a small bronze owl, along with a gas card and some cash." The agent explained.

"That was Raymond's bronze. Please give it to Lois when the police release the evidence."

"Yes, I will make sure. For now, ladies, I will say good-bye. I have an appointment at the Police Station to attend to." Marc kissed Laura on the forehead and shook Evelyn's hand.

"We'll meet up later, Marc." Laura said as he left.

Laura sipped her coffee and looked at Evelyn. "Evelyn, I love your sculpture, The Harmonious One. Can we talk about terms for a lay away? I didn't tell Marc yet, so this is just between us."

"OK, Laura. I'll need one thousand dollars down payment to hold it. The rest can spread out over sixteen months, at the most. That makes monthly payments of $250.00. Can you afford that?"

"Yes, I can do that. I brought my credit card to make the down payment."

"Let's go to my room and I'll write this agreement down for us to sign. I'll give you my address to mail payments." The two women left the restaurant and went to the 2nd floor hotel room.

Laura noticed more Native art on the walls of the hallway. Upon entering the room, she saw the sculpture sitting on the dresser. "There she is! Oh, she's so beautiful!"

"Yes, she is. She had many admirers at the Market.

I'm going to make a walnut pedestal that swivels for you. Since you are a teacher and I trust you, after the first twelve payments are made, we can arrange to meet and you can take her home. We can meet half-way, unless you want to drive to Third Mesa." Evelyn said.

"We'll see. Maybe Marc and I can drive out to see you. Otherwise, I'll meet you near Grants. Is that close enough for you?" asked Laura.

"That's perfect." Replied the artist.

Laura read the agreement and signed it. She gave the artist her credit card and the transaction was made. Laura got a receipt for her payment and the copy of terms. The two women shook hands.

Laura stroked the head of the sculpture and spoke softly. "I'll see you soon, Harmonious One."

"Thank you, Laura, for appreciating my work and for helping me through this period of mourning for my dear friend."

Laura gave the artist a hug and left the hotel room. She slowly roamed the halls of the hotel lobby admiring the artwork. She had the day off and thought of what she would do. She noticed that the Hotel had a Spa Center. She asked the Concierge if the Spa took walk-ins.

The Concierge made a call and told Laura she could have a foot message now, if she wanted. "That sounds perfect!" Laura was given directions and proceeded to the Spa. On the way, she passed a figure of a woman in bronze. The title was *Hopi Woman*. It was life-size and Laura looked at the face. It resembled Evelyn.

CHAPTER 20

Agent Bennett arrived at the Police Station just before his 11 a.m. meeting. He went to the Chief's office. There was a man sitting across from the Chief.

"Agent Bennett, this is Dr. Fred Smithson, the Forensic Psychiatrist I told you about." The men shook hands and the agent sat in the chair next to the doctor.

"I have the results of the suspect's blood test. He has high levels of Ketamine and Methamphetamine in his system. Ketamine alone can be an amnesiac and is abused for its hallucinogenic properties. It distorts perceptions of sights and sounds. The other drug, Meth, for short, can cause delusions, nonsense speech and memory problems. There was marijuana in his system, too."

"It sounds like his body is a chemistry lab." Said Chief Romero.

"In addition to the drugs, he's malnourished. His Electrolytes are off and he's dehydrated. The combination of the first two drugs can cause Substance-Induced Disorder, also known as SID. It appears, at this time, that your suspect has drug-induced Psychosis." Explained the doctor.

"What do you recommend, Doctor?" Asked agent Bennett.

"I think he should be hospitalized in a Psychiatric Ward. He should be confined to a bed in a private room with a guard placed nearby. As the drugs wear off, he'll need to be watched for seizures or other withdraw effects. He can be treated with an anti-psychotic medicine or a sedative during this time. For the first week, he would have an l.V. for fluids. After the first week, I'll re-assess his physical and mental state."

"Doctor, when shown the photo of the murder victim, the suspect said something relating to the murder scene. He said *white van*, which is where the murder occurred. The photo triggered his memory. He was, also, found with the victim's possessions on his body. His clothes were swabbed for blood and the DNA matches the victim's. Can this man stand trial for murder?" The agent inquired.

"He could not stand trial in this state. He has poor verbal skills, probably due to cognitive impairment. Since we don't know his history, we don't know his baseline condition before the drug use. We have to wait to observe his mental state when the drugs wear off." The doctor concluded.

"We don't even have his name yet. The library card found in his pocket had a name associated with another man, not resembling the suspect. We'll have to search Missing Persons database and see if his DNA matches anything we have in the system. We have to process this person. He has an arraignment today." Said Chief Romero.

"We'll have to refer to him as *John Doe*, for now. Inform the State District Attorney's office of the suspect's condition. Send these test results for reference and my expert recommendations." The doctor responded.

"He needs to be assigned a public defender. The attorney will meet his client before the arraignment so a plea can be entered. I doubt the judge will release him on bail, since he's a threat to the community." Agent Bennett explained.

"The State Prosecutor will tell the judge the suspect should be kept in a Psychiatric Ward. I'll call the hospital in town to see if they have a private room available. We need to get him out of the jail cell and into the hospital for treatment. I'll let you know when he can be transferred." The doctor stood up to leave.

"Doctor, can I make a copy of those lab results for the record?" Asked the Chief.

"Yes, of course." The two men left the office and Agent

Bennett stayed behind.

Agent Bennett dialed his FBI office. "Agent Garland, the suspect will be arraigned today. It's been advised that he be hospitalized in a Psychiatric Ward. He's been diagnosed with drug induced Psychosis and cognitive impairment. The state will charge him with murder."

"With the victim's possessions found on the suspect, as well as DNA from the victim's blood on his clothing and witness descriptions, he's facing Federal murder charges, as well. I will call the U.S. Attorney's Office. Since they prosecute federal crimes, the U.S. Marshals may want to keep him in their custody before trial."

"Another thing, Sir. We don't have his name. He can't tell us his name and the card in his possession belonged to someone else. We are referring to him as *John Doe.*"

"Then, the report will read *John Doe.*" Agent Garland hung up.

Chief Romero returned to his office with copies of the lab results. He handed a copy to Agent Bennett. "I'll call the State District Attorney's office and send them this report. When they see the suspect at the arraignment today, they will press the judge to follow the expert's plan for treatment. It remains to be seen if and when he can stand trial."

"I informed Agent Garland of the findings. He will file federal murder charges against *John Doe*, since it happened across state lines. I will notify Chief George Shunpavy." Agent

Bennett said.

"Chief, before I go, I'd like to address the homeless situation here. I think you should work with the Shelters and send Outreach to the hillside camp and along the river. You can clear out some of the people who don't do drugs first. Then, concentrate on the drug offenders. Otherwise, this could become a recurring problem for your city. Once the news gets out that a homeless drug addict killed a visiting artist, the residents are going to press you on the topic. By sending Outreach and the Night Ministry, you'll show that you are working on the problem."

"You're right, agent. I need to address this problem. It's a safety concern for the public, as well as the homeless. I can call the Directors of the City Shelters and direct an Outreach today at both locations. I'll convene a meeting with the Shelter Directors and the local aldermen this week." The Chief of Police continued. "I made a few calls to local businesses and got interviews for our two informants. I want to go tell them before I go to the arraignment."

The Chief rose from his desk chair and walked over to the agent. "Thanks for your help on this, agent." The two men shook hands.

Agent Bennett left the Station and walked to the downtown area. The rows of white booths were gone and local businesses displayed their *Open* signs for visitors to see. He went to the vacant office building on Marcy Street to see if the cardboard shelter was still in place. He saw an older man sitting in the corner amidst the pile of cardboard. His clothes were dirty and his face was burned red. There were holes in his shoes. The agent stood in front of the homeless man.

"Do you need help, sir?" The agent asked.

"No. I don't want any help." The man replied.

"Do you want to go to a Shelter? You will have a bed, a shower and food." The agent explained.

"I don't know. I don't know." The man said.

Agent Bennett sent a text to the Chief. "Send Outreach to corner of Otero and Marcy. Older man in building entry. Take him to shelter."

His phone pinged with a message back. "Got it!"

"Someone is coming to take you to a shelter, sir. Take care." The agent said.

Marc continued walking the downtown area this sunny afternoon. He looked at the boutiques, galleries and restaurant fronts. The Plaza had people sitting on benches, some eating ice cream cones. Families with young children laid on the grass. It all seemed a world away from life on the hillside.

CHAPTER 21

gent Bennett returned to his vehicle at the downtown Santa Fe Police Station. He dialed the number for the Hopi Tribal Police. "Chief George Shunpavy, please. Agent Bennett here."

A few minutes lapsed. "Hello, agent. Do you have an update for me?"

"Yes, Chief. We have the murder suspect in police custody. He had blood DNA from the victim, as well as some of his possessions. He fit the witness descriptions, as well. He was homeless, drug-induced and malnourished when we arrested him. When shown a photo of the victim, he said the words *white van*. We don't have his name yet, so is called *John Doe* for the record."

"Well, that's good work, agent. Did he admit to anything when questioned?" Asked the Chief.

"Chief, the man is cognitively impaired with poor verbal skills. He has a drug-induced Psychosis, based on his blood test and a doctor's diagnosis. He'll be arraigned today and faces state and federal murder charges. An expert recommends he be admitted to a Psychiatric Ward under guard to be observed during withdraw of the powerful drugs he's been on." The agent explained.

"Will you be the point person for this murder trial, agent?" Asked Chief Shunpavy.

"I can do that, Sir. Chief of Police for Santa Fe is Chief Romero and my Agent-in-charge is Agent Garland, with the FBI. I collaborate with the Santa Fe Police when needed."

"Do you think this man will be able to stand trial, agent?"

"He couldn't at this point, but that could change. If he can't stand trial, there's a state-owned Psychiatric Hospital in New Mexico that he may be admitted to. Since the man is facing federal charges, the U.S. Marshals may take custody. I will keep you informed." Agent Bennett explained.

"What a shame to lose such a valued member of our tribe. Raymond was not only a talented sculptor, he was a desert farmer who fed his people. He will be greatly missed, agent."

"Chief, Raymond tried to protect people by alerting others at Indian Market to the man's suspicious behavior. He gave a description of the suspect to others before he was killed.

His death, also, drew attention to the homeless population living in Santa Fe. Chief Romero is calling Shelter Directors to coordinate an Outreach Program today. They will have a meeting with city aldermen to address the problem later in the week."

"I have read about homeless populations in many cities across the U.S. Perhaps Raymond's death will shed more light on the situation." Replied Chief Shunpavy.

"A bit of good news, Chief. Before he was killed, Raymond submitted his bronze in a juried show at the Santa Fe Convention Center on Friday. The judges couldn't locate him to inform him Saturday that he won first place in sculpture, so they called Lois. She notified me that she wanted to come pick up his possessions and make burial arrangements."

"Well, that is some good news, agent Bennett. Raymond's artwork will get a high price with this prize and that will help take care of his mother and sister after his death. Raymond was always taking care of people. Do you know which sculpture won the prize?"

"Yes, *The Desert Farmer*."

CHAPTER 22

Laura Barnes felt more rejuvenated after her Spa treatment. She roamed the hotel grounds admiring the artwork by area American Indian artists. It was 3 p.m. She called Marc. "How is your day going?"

"Good timing, Laura. I just went to the suspect's arraignment to be sure he wouldn't be out on bail. The judge agreed he was a danger and should be hospitalized under guard. My work is finished here. What do you want to do?' Asked Marc.

"Let's have lunch and talk about those properties we saw yesterday. I'm at the hotel entrance." Laura said.

"I'll be there in 10 minutes."

Laura looked at her phone and dialed the number of a

Realtor she met yesterday. "We came by your Open House yesterday. Is there a chance we can visit later today, maybe 5 p.m.?" She asked.

"I'll call the owners to see if we can show on short-notice. I'll call you back." Replied the Realtor.

Marc pulled up to the hotel entrance and Laura entered the vehicle. "Any ideas for lunch?" He asked.

"I heard there's a bakery across the street that sells sandwiches and stuffed croissants. It's casual. Otherwise, there are places nearby in the Railyard District." Laura said.

"We can try the bakery. I'll park the car and we can walk across the street." Marc suggested.

The bakery was a short walk. Marc eyed the baked goods behind the glass counter. When asked what he wanted, he pointed to three different items. "What will you have, Laura?"

She pointed to a stuffed croissant and cookie. "Plus two lemonades, please." She said.

They found a table near the window looking out at Guadalupe Street traffic. They had just sat down, when Laura's phone rang. She recognized the number. "Yes, this is Laura." She listened. "OK. 5:15 it is. Thank you." She replied.

"Who was that?" Marc asked while eating his sandwich.

"Marc, we said we would talk about the properties we saw yesterday. What did you think about the first one on Rodeo Road?" Laura asked.

"The place was too small. We would outgrow it quickly."

Marc replied. "What about the other place near the IAIA Campus?"

"I liked it, but it was more money than I'd like to spend." Said Marc.

"What about the place on one acre in La Cienaga?" Laura asked.

"I liked the location, being closer to my office. The place had space and potential. It needs some updates, but that can happen over time. Of the three, that was my favorite. How about you?" he asked.

Laura finished chewing the bite of her croissant and smiled. "That was my favorite, too. I just made an appointment for us to go back and see it today while you're here."

"Really?" Marc asked. "That's rather presumptuous of you, but you're right. I think we should see it again since we both have the time today."

"We were in a hurry yesterday, so today we can take a closer look." Laura finished her lunch and looked at her watch. It was 4:00 p.m.

"Our appointment is at 5:15. Do you have anything else you want to do while you're here?"

"Let's drive by the Cross before we leave." Marc suggested.

They returned to his vehicle and drove down Guadalupe Street to Paseo de Peralta. Marc slowly drove past the famous Cross. The pathway up the hill was now filled with visitors taking photos of the country's oldest capital city. The high vantage point was a popular tourist spot.

"Chief Romero told the Shelters to do an Outreach on the hillside and along the river today."

"I hope some of those people take the offer for shelter. They need it or they may not survive." Laura said.

"The death of the visiting artist really shined a spotlight on the homeless situation here. The Chief is committed to working to solve this crisis." Marc continued driving along the Paseo and away from downtown Santa Fe.

"This is really a city of contrasts, isn't it? From ancient cultural traditions to modern science. Folk Art to high-end art galleries. Transient and homeless to the rich and famous." Laura said.

"Yes, the City Different is a very interesting place. Now, let's go see our possible future home!"

ABOUT THE AUTHOR

Linda A. Morton is a former educator for the Santa Fe Public Schools and former Art Tour Guide. She now lives in northern Illinois and tends her garden of native plants and vegetables. She is an avid reader of mystery novels. Her previous novel is High Desert Grave Robber, which also takes place in Santa Fe. She is a member of the New Mexico Book Association.